THE VAMPIRE TRICK

BOOK THREE IN THE VAMPIRE WISH SERIES

MICHELLE MADOW

DREAMSCAPE PUBLISHING

1

JACEN

"Princess Bianca?" Queen Laila stormed into my quarters, throwing the doors open with so much force that they banged against the walls. "You eliminated *Princess Bianca*? Without consulting me?"

I walked calmly over to the doors and shut them, turning around to face the furious queen. "The last I checked, this was my selection," I said. "Not yours."

"It might be your selection." Her voice was more level now, taking on an eerie chillness as she narrowed her eyes at me. "But it's *my* kingdom. You know how important this alliance is to the Vale. Or do I need to spell it out for you again?"

I sighed, because no, of course she didn't. I was well aware of the problem at hand. The Vale was situated deep in the Canadian Rocky Mountains. Centuries ago,

Queen Laila had journeyed to this location to build her vampire kingdom. Whens she'd arrived, the mountains were already habituated by shifters—people who could shift into the form of wolves. To prevent war, the wolves and Laila had signed a peace treaty. The treaty signed over a portion of the land to the vampires, while leaving the rest to the wolves. As long as the vampires didn't expand past their designated area, the treaty would remain in place.

Despite my disdain for the vampires—which I was full of, given that Queen Laila had turned me into one against my will—the vampires had kept our side of the treaty. The wolves, however, had been growing in numbers and strength. They'd recently decided they didn't *want* the vampires on "their" land anymore—they wanted to reclaim it all for themselves.

After centuries of peace, the vampires of the Vale had grown complacent. They weren't fit to fight against the growing numbers of the wolves. And so, Queen Laila had decided that the Vale needed an alliance with one of the other vampire kingdoms.

Preferably, with a kingdom of warriors.

The best way to form an alliance was through marriage. As the newest—and strongest—vampire prince of the Vale, I was the most eligible to make that alliance. So I went along with Queen Laila's plan and invited two princesses from each vampire kingdom to come to the Vale to seek my hand in marriage.

However, my motives didn't align with Queen Laila's.

I *wanted* the Vale to fall.

Queen Laila had taken everything from me when she'd sunk her fangs into my neck and turned me into a monster. When I'd first been turned, I'd lost control completely—I'd raided the village and drained countless humans dry. I didn't even remember how many people I'd killed.

All I knew was that I was surely doomed to Hell for what I'd done.

Any other vampire of the Vale would have been killed for losing control like that. Losing control of the bloodlust is considered too much of a liability for our species, and the punishment is a stake through the heart.

But not me.

Apparently Laila had been planning on turning me for a long time. As a human, I'd been a well-known athlete—I'd been training for the Olympic swim team, and had been predicted to win more gold medals than any swimmer in years.

But unbeknownst to me at the time, Laila had already chosen me to be her next prince. She'd been convinced that the strength I'd had as a human meant I would be an extraordinarily strong vampire.

So instead of killing me after I'd rampaged the village, she'd kept me alive, assigning extra guards to my quarters to ensure I didn't escape the palace again.

It had taken me nearly a year to gain control over my bloodlust.

I'd thought that once I proved I could control it, I would be free. But that wasn't the case.

I was only free to leave the palace walls and walk the streets of the vampire town and human village. The moment I'd left the Vale—with a human girl named Annika who I was helping escape—I'd been hunted down by wolves, vampires, *and* Camelia, the witch who upheld the Vale's boundary and acted as Laila's second in command.

I'd been sedated with wormwood—the only plant that acts like kryptonite to vampires—and brought back to the palace.

Annika had been killed.

Seeing her corpse made me realize that as long as Queen Laila was alive, I would *always* be a prisoner to her and the Vale. The vampire queen would never stop trying to control me.

I could only be free if Queen Laila was dead.

And so, I'd agreed to Queen Laila's plan to invite

vampire princesses from all over the world to the palace to seek my hand in marriage. But I hadn't agreed so I could help the Vale forge an alliance with one of the other kingdoms so we could stand stronger against the wolves.

I'd agreed so I could find a princess who would support a rebellion against Queen Laila and the Vale.

Now I had to convince Queen Laila that my decision to eliminate Princess Bianca was for the best interest of the Vale—despite the fact that Princess Bianca hailed from the Vale's greatest ally, the Carpathian Kingdom.

"Princess Bianca had the emotional capacity of an insect." I walked over to the sitting room, aware that this conversation wouldn't be short. But I couldn't sit down yet—as queen, Laila needed to sit first. Instead, I rested my hands on the back of the sofa, standing strong as I spoke. "She pales in comparison to Princess Karina."

Princess Karina was the other princess from the Carpathian Kingdom, and what I'd said was true. Princess Karina was intelligent and charming—everything that Princess Bianca was not.

"The Carpathian Kingdom cares about the Vale more than any other kingdom." Laila joined me in the sitting room, although she didn't take a seat. "King Nicolae cares for me deeply. Eliminating one of his princesses first was insulting."

"I didn't eliminate Princess Bianca first," I reminded her. "That honor would go to Princess Daniela of the Tower."

"Princess Daniela lost control of her bloodlust and attacked one of the humans in our village," Laila snapped. "You had no choice but to eliminate her."

"I *did* have a choice," I said. "I chose to eliminate Princess Daniela because it was what was best for the Vale. Which is the same reason why I eliminated Princess Bianca."

"You eliminated Princess Bianca because you didn't like her on a personal level," Laila said. "Not because it was beneficial to the Vale."

"It would hardly benefit the Vale for their prince to be married to a miserable—"

"Stop." Laila held a hand in the air, cutting me off before I could say what I truly thought of the cold-hearted princess. "What's done is done. In the future, however, you're to consult with me before eliminating another princess."

"I can't promise you that," I told her, and she narrowed her eyes, looking like she wanted to kill me then and there. "But I *can* promise not to eliminate Princess Karina without consulting you first."

"Will you make a blood oath on that promise?" she asked.

"I will." I walked over to my desk and opened the drawer, pulling out a knife and using it to make an incision on my palm. Once done, I handed the knife to Laila, who did the same.

We clasped hands, our palms connecting where the cuts bled.

"You promise me that you will not eliminate Princess Karina of the Carpathian Kingdom from the selection we're holding in the quest for your hand without consulting me first," Laila said, her eyes on me as she spoke. "Do you swear to agree to this blood oath?"

"I swear," I said, and my hand tingled, the magic binding me to my word.

We pulled our hands away, and our cuts sealed.

"Very well." Laila nodded and walked back to the sitting room, taking a seat on the sofa. "We have much to discuss, but let's jump to the most important matter first."

"Which matter is that?" I sat down in the sofa across from her, although I kept my posture stiff, not feeling comfortable enough to relax just yet.

"We need to discuss Princess Ana of the Seventh Kingdom."

2

JACEN

The mention of Princess Ana brought a tangle of emotions to my throat that I didn't quite understand.

Because Princess Ana reminded me of Annika, the human blood slave who had captured my attention last month and whose life I had failed to save. They weren't similar in looks—Princess Ana had red hair while Annika had dark hair, Ana had green eyes while Annika had brown, and Ana had freckles while Annika's skin was as smooth as porcelain.

It was the little things that reminded me of Annika. Like the way Princess Ana tilted her head when she waited for me to answer a question, the way they both were dedicated gymnasts, and the way they both refrained from drinking alcohol even during festive celebrations. Ana didn't think anyone noticed that she didn't touch her glass of champagne at the welcoming ball, but she was wrong.

I'd noticed.

But despite those similarities, the girls were also very different. Annika was fiery and open, while Ana was quiet and reserved. When I'd danced with Annika at the Christmas celebration in the village square—when I'd disguised myself as a human in the hope of feeling normal for a night—Annika had been quick to open up about her past and how she'd gotten to the Vale. Ana, on the other hand, revealed nothing about herself or where she came from. The conversations I'd had with Annika had flowed naturally and easily, while my attempts with Ana had been stilted and awkward.

Still, I refused to give up on Princess Ana just yet. There was something about her... something that made me want to give her a chance to open up.

I also knew that comparing her to Annika was futile. Because Annika was dead. She was never coming back.

I would never find out where the spark between us could had led.

"Have you learned more about the Seventh Kingdom?" I asked Laila, making sure I sounded as neutral as possible. I couldn't let Laila know that Princess Ana intrigued me as much as she did.

Laila was too quick to smash anything I cared about that didn't directly benefit herself.

"I've learned nothing," she said. "Neither have the leaders of the other kingdoms. Queen Mary of the Haven is even involving herself in the investigation, and she's come up empty handed as well."

"I thought the Haven represented neutrality and stayed out of political affairs?" I didn't know much more about the vampires of the Haven, other than that they fed off animal blood instead of human blood and that they allowed any non-royal vampire who was able to live in accordance to their diet to come live with them. Which wasn't easy, since animal blood only gave vampires about half the strength as human blood, but many were willing to do it in exchange for safety.

Oh, and also that they were protected by the tiger shifters who shared their land.

"The Haven is as invested in learning about another possible kingdom as much as anyone else," Laila said. "But like everyone else, they've been unable to discover any information."

"The Seventh Kingdom must be hidden exceptionally well," I said, finally feeling comfortable enough to lean back in my seat.

"Perhaps," Laila said. "Although it's far more likely that the Seventh Kingdom doesn't exist at all."

"Yet no vampire king or queen has claimed to have sired Princess Ana," I reminded her. "And Ana is clearly a princess, since she can use compulsion. She must come from *somewhere*."

"It doesn't add up," Laila agreed. "But the mysterious princess seems extremely taken by you. I see it in the way she looks at you. I was hoping you'd been able to glean some information from her about her kingdom."

Laila's comment took me by surprise. If Princess Ana seemed "taken" by me, I hadn't noticed it. Ana certainly didn't seem as taken by me as Princess Eve, who had invited herself to my bedroom after the welcome ball and had given herself to me for the taking.

I assumed Princess Eve meant for her actions to increase her chance at being chosen as my bride, but it had really done just the opposite.

"Princess Ana has revealed little about herself and nothing of her kingdom," I said, since it was the truth. "But I also want to learn more about the Seventh Kingdom. How would you feel about pushing up my date with Princess Ana to... tonight?"

Now that the welcome ball was complete, I was having individual dates with each of the princesses. So far, the only date that had taken place was the one with Princess Karina. Tonight was supposed to have been my date with Princess Bianca, but clearly that wouldn't be happening, since I'd eliminated her.

Anticipation rushed through my veins at the prospect of time alone with the mysterious Princess Ana instead.

"That would be too obvious of an insult to the princesses of the other kingdoms," Laila said. "But Princess Bianca's departure allows us to change the schedule around, and we should use that to our advantage. We'll recreate the schedule and place your date with Princess Ana in the middle. That way you can get information from her sooner, without giving her any obvious preference that might make the other princesses jealous."

"A fair deal," I agreed.

"But be careful about what you say around Princess Ana," Laila warned. "It's far more likely that she's up to something than that she's truly from a kingdom of myth."

"I know," I said, although I hoped Princess Ana was telling the truth. Mainly because I wanted to trust her, but also because of the possibility that the Seventh Kingdom might want to help me in my mission to take down the Vale.

"In the meantime, it's best to keep her here," Laila

said. "At least here, we have an eye on her and can discover who she is and where she comes from."

"I'll do everything I can to uncover the truth," I said, although my reasons for wanting to do so were very different from Laila's.

Because if Princess Ana *was* trying to harm the Vale, I would do everything I could to help her succeed.

3

ANNIKA

I WALKED through the hall of the palace with a book tucked under my arm, heading to the library.

The Vale operated on a nocturnal schedule—everyone was awake at night and slept during the day. The schedule was to accommodate the vampires, who were weakened in the sunlight. It had been a tough adjustment, but I'd gotten used to it since being kidnapped to the Vale about a year ago to be a blood slave in the human village.

In the human village, I'd worked at a bar called the Tavern, serving the standard fare of chicken, rice, beans, and watered down beer to humans on their breaks from work. I'd had time to read at the end of the day, but not much—unless I stayed up later than I should have to finish a book I couldn't put down. Which, to be honest, happened more often than I cared to admit. I'd simply been glad that while humans weren't allowed to have television or internet, we *were* allowed to read books. I hadn't been much of a reader before being kidnapped to the Vale—my life had always been packed with school, gymnastics practice, and homework—but with only books available to the humans of the Vale for entertainment, I'd quickly learned what I'd been missing out on.

Now that I was disguised as a vampire princess and had my own quarters in the palace as "Princess Ana," I had less to do in my waking hours than ever. And so, I'd been thrilled when my guard Tess had shown me the royal library. It contained way more books than the small bookshop in the human village could ever imagine. And unlike the books in the human village—which were worn, torn, and had smudged pages—the books in the palace library were fresh and new.

In the human village, I'd been in the middle of reading a popular series—so popular that there were theme parks built after it. It had been easy to find the book that I'd left off on so I could get back into the story.

I'd just finished the book and was bringing it to the library to return it and grab the next one when I ran into Prince Jacen in the hallway.

He was dressed casually, in jeans and a button down

shirt. It was the most casual I'd seen him since I'd arrived to the Vale as Princess Ana. It reminded me of the first time I'd met him—when he'd snuck into the village in disguise as a human.

I'd liked the person I'd thought he was that night. More than liked—I'd been instantly attracted to him.

But that person had never existed.

"Princess Ana." He stopped walking. His eyes traveled from my face, to the book in my hand, and then back to my face. "I see you've discovered our library?"

"Yes," I said, bringing the book in closer to my chest. I searched for something else to add, but came up with nothing.

Why did my brain go haywire every time I was in his presence?

My guard Tess stepped aside and looked away from us, clearly trying to give us as much privacy as possible.

"I'm on my way to return a book." It was stating the obvious, but at least it was better than saying nothing.

"I see that." He looked again to the book I was holding. "I've seen the movies—haven't read the books."

"They're amazing," I told him. "I didn't read much as a human—I was always so busy—but since being turned into a vampire I've had much more time on my hands. I can't believe I didn't read this series sooner."

"I think that's the most you've told me about yourself

since you arrived to the palace," he said with a smile. "Would you like me to escort you to the library?"

"If you want to," I told him. "I don't want to keep you if you have somewhere important to be…"

"Nothing's more important than spending time with the princesses who have journeyed here to get to know me," he said, starting toward the library. "Come. Let's walk."

I did as he said, not having much of a choice.

We walked in silence for a few seconds, and I searched my mind for something to say. I'd never had a problem talking with him as Annika—back then, it had seemed like I was always bursting with questions for him. But as Princess Ana, it was different. I was afraid of saying something that might blow my cover.

Taking on a new identity was much harder than I'd anticipated.

How had Jacen done such a good job of it when he'd pretended to be human that night in the village?

I could only guess it was because he was a born liar. Anger filled me at the reminder of his betrayal. He'd shown his true colors by lying to me, convincing me he cared about helping me escape, and then leaving me for dead.

I, on the other hand, always liked to be honest. But honesty was impossible when I was lying about who I was, which left me at a loss of what to say. However, my silence certainly wouldn't help me in my goal to get Prince Jacen to keep me here as long as possible so I could learn how to kill Queen Laila. And I could already see the entrance to the library, so I needed to say *something*.

"Do you come here often?" I finally asked, at the same time as he said, "I'm switching around the nights of the dates."

We stopped walking, our eyes meeting as we exchanged awkward smiles.

"Do I come here often?" he repeated my question, chuckling. "I *live* here."

"I meant to the library." I turned my eyes down, my cheeks heating. "Never mind. What were saying about the nights of the dates?"

"Due to Princess Bianca's departure, I've switched around the order of the dates." He straightened, clearly back to business. "Instead of next week, your date with me will be on Thursday night."

"Wow," I said. "That's… soon."

"I was hoping you would be more excited than that," he said.

"I am!" I assured him. "I'm just nervous, is all."

"Don't be," he said smoothly. "These dates are so we

can get to know each other. I want you to be comfortable."

"It's hard to be comfortable in those fancy dresses I have to wear at each meal." The comment came out before I realized what I was saying, and I squirmed, embarrassed by my mistake.

What kind of princess complained about having to wear fancy dresses? He was going to think the Seventh Kingdom was barbaric.

Not like it mattered, since the Seventh Kingdom didn't exist at all.

"I couldn't agree more." He smiled again—a real smile that reached his eyes. "If you don't show up on Thursday night dressed comfortably, I'll be extremely disappointed."

"So I can wear jeans?" I asked.

"If that's what you're most comfortable in, then you *better* wear jeans," he said.

"Challenge accepted." I returned his smile with one of my own, surprised at how easy it had been to slip into friendly conversation with him.

"Good," he said. "I'm looking forward to it. And to answer your question—yes, I do come to the library often. Although I rarely read fiction."

"Non-fiction, then," I assumed. "About what?"

Given his history as an athlete, I guessed he liked to read about sports.

"History," he said, the answer taking me by surprise. "Mainly the history of the Vale, although I read as much about the supernatural world as possible. The library here is one of the few places in the world with accurate information about supernatural history. I assume the library of the Seventh Kingdom has similar books as well?"

"Of course," I lied, not wanting the Seventh Kingdom to sound primitive.

At the same time, I realized how stupid I was being by spending my free time reading fiction. I was here to overthrow the Vale.

A good place to start would be by learning as much about it as possible.

"Well, I have to be going." Jacen reached for the library door and opened it for me. "It was a pleasure running into you, Princess Ana."

"Thank you," I told him, stepping through the door. "It was a pleasure running into you, too."

The door closed, and I stared around at the library, taking a few breaths to get ahold of myself. That conversation with Jacen had been so *easy*. It reminded me of the time I'd spent with him as Annika.

But beneath the good looks and charm, he was

selfish and cold-hearted. He was an extraordinarily good actor, but I couldn't let myself forget who he *truly* was, no matter what.

And so, I slipped the novel I'd been carrying into the return slot and headed to the non-fiction section of the library.

Because I had a kingdom to overthrow.

4

ANNIKA

THE BOOKS on supernatural history were all written by hand, and I wasn't allowed to check them out. It looked like I would be spending my afternoon in the library.

I was engrossed in multiple books spread out over the table when a shadow loomed overhead.

I looked up and saw four of the princesses—Eve, Margaret, Darra, and Tari. Two of them were from Utopia—the all female kingdom in New Zealand, and two were from the Ward—the warrior kingdom in West Africa. They towered over me, their arms crossed and their lips set in firm lines as they stared down at me.

My heart leaped into my throat. I didn't know why they were here, but it couldn't be good. And I couldn't help thinking about whoever had been trying to sabotage me since my arrival—the person who had made sure Tess didn't know to tell me about the talent I needed to show during the welcome ball, and who had slipped a note with "go home" written in blood under my door at some point while I'd been sleeping last night.

By the way the four princesses were looking at me, I wouldn't have been surprised if it was one of them. Or *all* of them.

"Did you want to use this table?" I asked, even though all of the other tables in the section were empty.

"No." Eve stepped forward—apparently she was the leader of the group. "We wanted to talk to you."

"All right." I was relieved that they wanted to talk, since they were looking at me like they wanted to beat me up. I closed up the books and stacked them into a pile. "Would you like to sit?"

"No." One of the twins snarled—I assumed Tari, since she was the more vocal of the two. "You should have stood the moment you saw us, given our ranks."

"We're the same rank." I tried to keep my voice steady, not wanting to give away how intimidated they were making me feel. I glanced to the front of the library, relieved at the sight of Tess standing with four other guards—I assumed the guards for the four princesses. Tari and Darra were both skilled warriors—they could probably beat the guards in a fight—but it made me feel better to know I was protected.

Well, *physically* protected. The guards couldn't stop the princesses if they attacked me verbally. Which was exactly what I felt like they were preparing to do right now.

"We're *not* the same rank," Eve said, her nose in the air. "The four of us are princesses."

"As am I," I reminded them, trying to keep my voice as calm as possible. A princess didn't raise her voice—right? "You all saw me use compulsion on our first day here, as did the rest of the court."

"We did." Eve nodded. "But we're princesses of actual kingdoms. *Your* kingdom doesn't exist. The Seventh Kingdom is a myth. Therefore, you're a princess of nothing and should rise in our presence."

"I will not." I leaned back in my chair and crossed my arms, making it clear I wasn't budging.

The thing was, they were right. I was further from a vampire princess than they could imagine. If they knew what I really was—a human blood slave—they would kill me here and now.

But I was sick and tired of vampires pushing me around. So I was staying in this chair, even if all four of them tried to pull me out of it themselves.

"You should have been the one sent home this morning." Eve sneered. "Not Princess Bianca."

"I thought you would be happy that Princess Bianca

was gone." I held my gaze steady with hers. "It means there's one less princess for us to compete against."

"We'll be happy once *you're* gone," Princess Margaret chimed in. "You're wasting the time of our prince."

"*Your* prince?" I laughed. "Prince Jacen belongs to no one."

"He belonged to me after the ball." Eve smirked and tossed back her hair, watching me as she waited for my reaction.

I prickled, but tried to keep the annoyance from my face. "What do you mean by that?" I asked, each word crisp and steady.

"Once the ball was over, he invited me to his quarters," she said. "As for what happened once we were there, use your imagination. Which it sounds like you have a lot of, since you used it to invent an entire kingdom."

Margaret laughed and moved closer to Eve. The twins showed no emotion whatsoever. They were unreadable—like statues.

I didn't want to believe what Eve had said. But I also remembered the way Jacen had looked at her on the night of the ball. He'd been attracted to her—there was no doubt about it.

He'd always behaved like a gentleman around me, but then again, Jacen was a cold-hearted liar. And Eve looked so smug that my gut told me she was telling the truth.

I couldn't let the one good conversation I'd had with Jacen in the hallway earlier make me get soft toward him. If I allowed myself to get swayed by such a small thing, how was I supposed to be strong enough to pull off my mission?

"I'm leaving," I told the princesses, standing up from my chair with so much force that it nearly toppled over behind me.

"You're leaving the palace?" Eve quirked an eyebrow. "That's the most sensible thing you've said since you arrived."

"I'm not leaving the palace." I narrowed my eyes at her and squared my shoulders, glad that I was taller than her in Ana's body. "I'm returning to my quarters. The only way I'll be leaving the Vale is if Prince Jacen asks me to leave himself."

I turned around and walked away from them, not bothering once to look behind.

5

ANNIKA

I SOMEHOW MANAGED to wait until reaching my quarters before collapsing onto my bed and bursting into tears.

I hated that I was crying over such a stupid confrontation. It was obvious from the start that those girls didn't like me—they hadn't tried to hide it.

But the girls weren't all I was crying over. While I hated to admit it, the thought of Jacen and Eve together hurt. Why had he taken the most hateful princess of the whole bunch to his bed? The only princess who'd been nice to me so far was Princess Isabella, but she was quiet and generally kept to herself. She was also my competition. They *all* were. I couldn't let myself forget that.

I was alone here. I was alone *everywhere*.

There was no one left in the world who cared about me. And it was all the fault of the vampires.

Someone sat on the bed, and I looked up, finding Geneva. Not in her true form, of course—the others in the palace would have recognized her true form. Instead, she was using a transformation potion to appear as a homely middle-aged woman. While in the palace, she was posing as my lady's maid, and she'd taken up the room connected to mine.

All on my command, of course. As long as I had possession of Geneva's sapphire ring—which I'd been keeping in a hidden pocket of my underwear—she was bound to do as I commanded.

"Since you're not volunteering anything, I guess I'm going to be forced to ask you." She sighed and rolled her eyes, her brazen attitude coming through despite her modest form. "What happened?"

I sat up, sniffed, and wiped the tears from my face. Once in control of myself, I gave her a run-down of what had happened in the library.

"I hate her," I said once I was done.

"Which one?" Geneva asked.

"Eve."

"Why?" She raised an eyebrow. "Because she confronted you about the Seventh Kingdom not being real, or because she slept with your silver-eyed prince?"

I glared at her. Next time I was upset, I needed to

remember that Geneva was *not* a good source of comfort.

"Forget about it." I sighed and sat back into the pillows. "I just wish supernaturals didn't exist, and that I was home with my family like I should be."

"I'm afraid my powers don't extend that far," Geneva said. "I can't kill people or bring back the dead."

"I know." I huffed. "It was a figure of speech. I wasn't making a *real* wish."

"Be specific in your language in the future," she told me. "The spell that binds me doesn't take these 'figures of speech' into account."

"Will do," I said, although now that I was reminded of my wishes, I wanted to do *something* to get back at those princesses. Mainly, Eve. "Would it be in your power to give Eve a horrible case of acne?"

"Technically, yes," Geneva said. "Except that vampires don't experience such human ailments. If Princess Eve were to come down with acne, she would know that a witch had cast a spell upon her. And since you're the only vampire princess with a witch as her lady's maid…"

"She'll suspect that I'm the one who did it," I said. "Any spell cast on *any* of the princesses will likely be blamed on me."

"Yes," Geneva agreed. "Even though you're

masquerading as a princess, you should behave like a queen. A queen doesn't best her competition by lowering herself to the petty tactics of schoolgirls. A queen bests her competition by *being* the best."

"How are you such an expert on queens?" I asked her.

"I've known one or two of them in my time." She glanced at the door, her eyes far off, and then snapped her attention back to me. "My personal opinion is that queens are always far better rulers than kings."

I was about to say that Queen Laila didn't fit that pattern, but it seemed stupid to voice such a thought while in her palace. My quarters *felt* private, but I couldn't allow myself to get too comfortable. I had no idea who might overhear.

"I wish for you to create a sound barrier," I told Geneva. "So that no one can overhear our conversation. *That's* within your power, right?"

"Most certainly." She flicked her hand. "The sound barrier is up. You may speak freely now."

"Good," I said. "Because I've been doing a lot of thinking about why I'm here."

"You've changed your mind about wanting to rid the world of Laila?" Geneva asked.

I couldn't be certain, but it almost seemed like her eyes lit up at the prospect.

"No," I said quickly, since there was no question in

my mind—Laila had destroyed the lives of too many humans. Her reign needed to end. "But I *am* worried about the feasibility of this plan."

"What about it?" Geneva asked.

"The current plan is that I pretend to be a vampire princess, get Prince Jacen to propose to me, marry him, and then kill Queen Laila once I'm an official princess of the Vale," I started.

"Yes." Geneva nodded. "That's what we discussed."

"But I'm already here," I said. "And we can't say for sure that Prince Jacen will choose me. So why not kill Queen Laila *now*?"

"Because with princesses from all over the world staying here, security is higher than ever," Geneva said, her eyes sharp. "Now is the *worst* time to launch an attack on the queen. You'll fail."

"I thought you were the most powerful witch in the world?" I challenged. "Surely if anyone can help me pull this off, it's you?"

"I'm the most powerful witch in the world, but I'm not stupid," she snapped. "Launching an attack when Laila is expecting it is stupid. You would be dooming yourself to fail."

"But at least I'm here and can get a shot at her," I pointed out. "If Jacen eliminates me from the competition and I have to leave the palace, I'll have lost my chance entirely."

"So don't get eliminated from the competition." She said it like it was the simplest thing in the world.

"Easier said than done."

We glared at each other, and I had a feeling we'd reached a standstill.

"You're letting Eve get you worked up for nothing," Geneva said, calmer now. "I've seen enough of men to know that the prince won't choose a quiff like her."

"I don't know," I said, defeated. "But at the rate things are going, he won't choose me, either. And if I get eliminated and lose my chance to take down Laila, I'll regret it for the rest of my life."

"If you try to take down Laila when security is so heightened, you won't be alive to regret anything," she said. "Neither will I, for that matter. The guards will kill you before you can get within arms length of the queen. If you're killed while wearing my ring, the ring will go dormant and I'll be gone, too. I'm looking out for myself just as much as I'm looking out for you."

"I know." I sighed and ran my fingers through my hair, since she *did* have a point. "But it sounds like you're looking out for Queen Laila, too."

"I'm looking out for myself," she repeated, her voice

hard. "And as long as my ring is tied to your life, that means I'm looking out for you as well."

"I know." I felt like we were going in circles now. "I guess I thought we would start forming the plan to kill Laila the moment we got to the palace. I even tried reading about the Vale today while in the library, and I couldn't find anything that might help."

"Queen Laila isn't so foolish as to keep the key to killing her in a book in the library." Geneva smirked again.

From the way she spoke of Laila, it sounded like she admired her.

"No." I crossed my arms, feeling more frustrated than ever. "But it didn't hurt to try. Better than sitting around all day waiting and doing nothing."

"You're impatient," Geneva observed. "But killing an original vampire is no easy business. The originals have always been secretive—it's what's kept them alive for all these centuries."

"You don't know how to kill her," I realized. "That's why you're stalling."

"Like I said, this is no easy business." Her lack of a direct answer verified that I was correct. "But I will come up with a plan—one that will keep you alive. All I ask is that you bide the time until I do and make sure that the prince keeps you in this competition. Can you do that?"

I opened my mouth, ready to say that I would try. But I closed it, remembering a quote from Star Wars that my brother always reminded me of whenever I was struggling with a new skill in gymnastics—"Do or do not. There is no try."

My date with Jacen was coming up this week. It was up to *me* to make sure it went well enough that he would choose to keep me in the Vale. I had no idea how to do that—dating had never been a skill of mine, since I'd always been so focused on schoolwork and gymnastics that I hadn't had time for dating.

But Jacen had been interested in me enough as Annika, and our conversation in the hallway earlier had gone well. In the hallway, I'd been acting more like myself than I had since arriving to the palace. Maybe that was the trick—I needed to act more like myself.

I could do this. I *had* to do this.

"Yes," I told her, trying to sound as confident as I wanted to feel. "I can."

6

KARINA

The wolf—a boy who couldn't have been older than sixteen—turned around and ran toward the town. Like the others, he didn't smell of wolf thanks to the concealment charm the witch Marigold had created for him.

"That's the final one?" I asked Noah, who stood with Marigold across the boundary.

I couldn't believe I was helping the wolves sneak into the Vale. But King Nicolae was convinced that if the Vale fell, Queen Laila would have no where else to turn but to him—and that she would finally be his queen like he'd always wanted. When the invitation from Prince Jacen had arrived requesting that two princesses be sent to the Vale from each vampire kingdom, King Nicolae had been quick to select me. Not because he wanted me to win Prince Jacen's heart—but because he wanted me to work from the inside to help the wolves take down the kingdom.

King Nicolae's unrequited obsession with Queen Laila didn't faze me. The only thing I cared about was the blood oath he'd made me—his promise that if I helped the wolves take down the Vale and got Laila to him, he would do everything he could to get me Geneva's sapphire ring. He was positive that Laila had the ring. Whether or not she did didn't bother me—by the terms of the blood oath, Nicolae was bound to help me get the ring if I helped take down the Vale and brought Laila to him.

I *needed* that ring. Geneva was the only witch in the world who could have strong enough powers to resurrect the love of my life, Peter.

I would do anything to have Peter back.

Even if that meant turning against my own kind and fraternizing with the enemy.

"He's the final one," Noah confirmed, his gaze locked on mine.

For a wolf, I found Noah strangely agreeable. All I'd known of wolves before coming to the Vale were the savage packs that prowled the boundary of the Carpathian Kingdom—the castle in the Carpathian Mountains of Eastern Europe where I'd lived since King Nicolae had taken me from my Romanian town over a century ago and turned me into a vampire princess. The wolves around our castle were animalistic and vicious.

According to Noah, the packs in the Vale used to war all the time, too. Then they'd started receiving visions in their dreams—prophecies that told them their Savior was ready to rise and bring peace to their kind.

The only catch? Their Savior could only rise if the vampires were cleared from the Vale.

I wasn't sure what I thought of the supposed prophecies. All I knew was that Noah was the first to receive the dream, and that from the passionate way he talked about his cause, he truly believed in what he was doing by bringing the wolves together in preparation to defeat the vampires.

Not like that mattered to me, of course.

All that mattered was getting Peter back.

"Now we just have to wait for the scouts to complete their job," Marigold said, her eyes gleaming as she looked out to the spot where the most recent wolf had disappeared into the forest.

Marigold was a witch who used to live in the Carpathian Kingdom. When King Nicolae learned that the wolves outside of the Vale were becoming a threat to Queen Laila, he'd sent Marigold to investigate. While investigating, Marigold had fallen in love with the leader of Noah's pack, Cody. Now, Marigold was fully invested in helping the wolves in their cause.

With my help, she'd used her powers to sneak a few wolves into the boundary for a scouting mission.

"Is that all you need from me?" I asked, looking back and forth between Marigold and Noah. My gaze eventually settled on Noah. I couldn't help it—even though he was a wolf, he was remarkably attractive. I would never say it out loud, of course, but there was something magnetic about him.

Perhaps it was because he had such a passionate belief in his cause. I'd always found passion to be attractive. It was what had drawn me to Peter back at the turn of the twentieth century—Peter had been just as interested and passionate about the technological advancement of mankind as I.

I'd lost that passion after he died. King Nicolae was known for being stuck in his ways, and I'd allowed myself to become trapped in time along with the rest of the Carpathian Kingdom.

Progress reminded me too much of Peter. And being reminded of the love that I'd lost was too much to bear.

"It's all we need for now," Noah said. "But there is one more thing I'd be honored for you to do for us."

"What's that?" I tapped my foot, since I didn't have all day. I'd piled on layers of clothing so I could sneak out of the palace during the day, but the sun weakened my strength. The sooner I returned to the palace, the more time I would have to recover before everyone awoke at sunset.

"I'd like for you to come with me to camp and meet the pack."

"What?" I backed up, looking at him like he was crazy. "No. No way. This was never part of our agreement."

"Our agreement was that you would help us defeat the vampires," Marigold chimed in. "Between the first time you came to us and now, members of the pack have been receiving more dreams. The dreams tell them that when it's time to bring down the Vale, they'll have the help of a witch and a vampire. I'm the witch. Seeing you —the vampire—will show them that the time for our Savior to rise is approaching."

"The visions have really been showing that?" I looked to Noah for confirmation. He'd been the first wolf to receive a vision—they called him the First Prophet. I trusted him with this more than I trusted Marigold.

He wouldn't lie about something so important to him.

"They have." He nodded. "The wolves have been doubtful that a vampire would ever help our cause. A few are even starting to desert camp. Seeing you would put their fears to rest and solidify the packs once more."

"They'll be thrilled to meet you," Marigold added, stepping up next to Noah.

"If they don't jump on me and attack me first," I muttered.

I could take on wolves in a fight—I'd done it before—but walking into a camp full of multiple packs while weakened by sunlight would be a suicide mission.

"They won't harm you," Noah assured me. "They only want proof of your existence. I'll return you safely to the Vale before sunset. You have my word."

"Are you willing to make a blood oath on that promise?" I asked.

"I will," he told me. "As long as you agree to tell no one of our location."

"All right," I said, satisfied with his response. "We'll make the blood oath. And then I'll go with you to the camp."

7

KARINA

I STEPPED out of the boundary, into air that was brisk and cold. It was the type of weather I'd expected during winter in the Canadian Rockies. The witch of the Vale—Camelia—kept the inside of the boundary warm, assumedly so the humans wouldn't freeze. As a vampire, the cold didn't bother me, and it didn't bother Noah, either. Since Marigold wasn't bundled up to the extreme, I guessed she was using a spell to keep herself warm.

"You should wear this." Marigold held a small brown pouch out to me. There was a cord attached to it so the wearer could put it around his or her neck.

"What is it?" I asked.

"An enchanted mixture of herbs and spices," she said.

"It's an extra of what I gave to the wolves we sent inside the boundary. It'll hide your scent."

I took it from her and put it around my neck, since she was right—going into a camp full of wolves without hiding my vampire scent would be asking for trouble.

Noah led the way to the camp. The two of us ran, and he carried Marigold on his back, since witches didn't have the speed of shifters and vampires. I was slower than usual, due to the sunlight weakening my strength, but Noah kept a pace that I could maintain.

We must have run for twenty miles before a wolf stopped us in our path. The animal growled at me, its lips pulled back to show its teeth.

I looked around for a weapon, ready to fight if necessary. There were plenty of sticks and stones nearby. Of course, since it was only one wolf, I could fight well enough with my hands and fangs, but better to be safe than sorry.

Noah placed his arm in front of me—a clear sign for the wolf not to attack. "The outsider is no threat," he said to the wolf. "She's the vampire from our visions, here to help us win back our land."

The wolf shifted into human form. He was another man—not quite as tall as Noah, but much more muscular. I assumed he was some kind of guard.

"It's true, then?" he asked, looking at me. "A vampire is going to help us in our cause?"

"Yes." I nodded. "I helped Marigold sneak the final scout through the boundary today."

"Scout." He snorted. "That's one word for it. But all right—I believe you. Only because no other vampire in their right mind would volunteer to come to our camp otherwise."

"I've brought her here to introduce her to the pack, so they can see for themselves that the visions are coming true," Noah said.

"Very well." The wolf turned his attention to me once more. "Do you have a name, vampire?"

"Daria." I used the name of my long-dead sister—the sister I'd had when I'd been a human. While I trusted Noah enough to let him take me here, I certainly didn't trust the wolves enough to provide them with my true identity.

"All right, Daria," he said with a nod. "I'll escort the three of you to camp to make sure no other guards bother you on your way in."

He turned around and led the way.

8

KARINA

THE CAMP WAS MORE normal than I'd expected.

Clusters of tents were set up all around, and in the middle of the clusters were campfires with blankets. Families gathered around the fires, cooking, making clothes, and chatting amongst themselves. Many were also forging weapons—stakes, for the most part. Farther away, wolves trained for battle, using both weapons and teeth.

"You look surprised," Noah observed, his eyes shining with pride when he looked at me.

"I didn't expect it to be this... civilized," I admitted.

"It wasn't this way until recently," he told me. "Before the packs came together—when we were constantly at war—we remained in our wolf forms as much as possible. We slept as wolves, ate as wolves, and fought as wolves. But we're shifters—we're not pure animals. We're meant to be human, too. By coming together, we've been able to set up camp and satisfy our human sides as well."

"But you're not human," I said. "Shifters feed on humans, just as vampires do."

The only difference was that humans could survive a vampire bite if we didn't drain them dry. Once a wolf took a chomp of a human, that human was as good as dead.

"The more time we spend in our wolf form, the less in touch we get with our humanity," he explained. "The wolf takes over, and humans become prey, like any other prey out there. It's something shifters have struggled with since the beginning of time. For centuries, our packs have been more wolf than human. But the dreams have brought us together and encouraged us to embrace our humanity once more. Once our Savior rises, we hope to make this camp more permanent. Perhaps we'll even integrate with society. On the outskirts, of course —our wolves will always need the opportunity to run free—but with the peace and salvation brought by our Savior, integration should finally be possible."

"Well, at least I wasn't *totally* wrong in thinking that the shifters were complete animals," I said. "I hope your Savior brings you the peace you're looking for."

"I didn't peg you as the type to admit to being wrong about anything." Noah smirked. "But since you said it first, I can admit as well—I suppose that my assumption about all vampires being soulless and cold-hearted was wrong, too."

I smiled at him, glad we could agree about *something*.

Then I realized that I actually felt a connection between us, and I averted my eyes, gazing around the camp to distance myself from him once more.

"If you're not animals, what's that cage for?" I glanced at a half-built cage in the distance, where men were working to complete the structure.

"It's for Laila." He omitted her title, like he did for all royal vampires. "Original vampires can't be killed as easily as most vampires—they can only be killed by Nephilim. They're impervious to all other attacks."

"Where did you hear that?" I asked, surprised that he knew.

After the last Nephilim had been killed, royal vampires had used compulsion to compel that knowledge from anyone who knew. The original vampires kept their secret from most everyone. For reasons of self-preservation, they didn't want the word to get out on how they could be killed. I only knew because I was in King Nicolae's trusted circle—I was one of the vampires who had used my compulsion to hide that knowledge from the rest of the supernatural world.

"Our Savior told us in our dreams," he answered, his words giving me chills.

These dreams must be legitimate if they contained the knowledge of how to kill an original vampire.

"Your Savior is correct," I told him. "But I hardly think a wooden cage will be enough to contain Queen Laila."

"It will once I have my way with it," Marigold piped in from behind us. I'd forgotten she was even there until now. "We'll infuse the wood with wormwood, and I'll use my magic to intensify the plant's effect. It'll weaken her so much that she won't have the strength to escape. Not like she'll be conscious to try, since we'll inject her with wormwood as well."

I shuddered and looked away from the cage, hating to imagine any vampire trapped inside of such a torture device.

"The plan has already been arranged with King Nicolae," Marigold continued. "Once Laila is captured, he'll receive a call to come get her. He'll bring two witches, both with enough magic to teleport them back to the Carpathian Kingdom."

"And the king is going to do what?" I asked. "Keep

Laila as a prisoner in the castle until she agrees to be his queen?"

The question was rhetorical—of course no one knew what King Nicolae would do with Laila. But with her kingdom destroyed and her title ripped from under her, the possibilities were endless. I didn't think he would hurt her, but he was so obsessed with her that he might keep her in the castle against her will.

"What he does with her is his business," Noah said, strong and sure. "All that matters is that once the vampires are cleared from the Vale, our Savior will finally be free to rise."

And once King Nicolae has Laila where he wants her, he'll get me Geneva's sapphire ring and I can wish for Peter's return, I thought, although I didn't voice it out loud.

We stood there for a few seconds in silence, and I took in the scene around me.

"You didn't have to use a fake name," Noah said in my ear, softer now. "You can trust me to keep you safe."

My heart leaped into my throat at how close he was standing, and I forced myself to take a step back. "I know you'll keep me safe," I told him, and I meant it. "But I wanted to be careful… in case something goes wrong, I can't risk having my identity known. It's best they think I'm a regular vampire of the Vale."

"Nothing about you is regular." His eyes were intense

as he gazed at me. "You're royalty, and it shows in your every movement."

"Thank you." I gave an exaggerated curtsy, hoping to lighten the tension between us. "Perhaps I'll be 'Lady Daria' then? Not a princess… but not a commoner, either."

"Lady Daria it is." He held a hand out to me. "But we've been standing on the periphery for far too long. Come. It's time to introduce you to the pack."

9

KARINA

It took only five minutes for Noah and Marigold to assemble the wolves. Soon, the three of us were standing atop a picnic table, the wolves gathered around us.

"Over the past few days, our Savior has been sending us new dreams—dreams that say we'll be able to fight the vampires and win once a witch and a vampire join our cause." Noah projected his voice so loudly that even the wolves in the back could hear. "You all are familiar with the witch Marigold, mate to my pack leader Cody." At the mention of Marigold's name, cheers erupted in the crowd.

I stopped myself from making a face at the reference of her as his "mate." Wolves weren't supposed to mate with anyone outside of their species. I'd never *heard* of such a thing. But from the way the wolves were cheering, I supposed they found nothing wrong with it—they seemed to accept Marigold as one of their own.

"Now, the second part of the prophecy is coming true," Noah continued once the cheering quieted. He looked to me, his eyes full of happiness. "I present Lady Daria of the Vale!"

He lifted the charm off my neck, and the crowd gasped as my vampire scent was let loose. A few wolves looked at me with skepticism, but for the most part, they were stunned into silence, appearing awed by my presence.

"Daria has been helping Marigold and I sneak the volunteers into the Vale," Noah continued. "She's been instrumental to our cause."

"Why?" someone shouted from the crowd—a female wolf who looked to be in her thirties. A few wolves nodded in agreement. "Why would a vampire help our cause?"

Everyone looked to me for my answer—including Noah.

I couldn't tell them my real reason, so I needed to come up with something else. Fast. Something based on Noah's story that I was a vampire of the Vale—not a princess from the Carpathian Kingdom.

"I was turned into a vampire against my will," I answered quickly. Prince Jacen had recently told me of his experience in the Vale—he seemed to be harboring a lot of animosity toward the way things were done there. And the best lies were always based on the truth. I would simply use his truth as my lie. "The vampires of the Vale took my life from me. I'll never be able to see my family again, because they'll never accept me for what I am now. I'm as good as dead to them." That part, I took from my own story. "I never *wanted* to be like this." I spoke stronger now, noticing that the wolves were rapt as they listened. "Because of the vampires of the Vale, I'm condemned to be a monster forever. They can't keep getting away with turning humans into vampires against their will. They have to pay for what they've done. You all—the wolves who should rightfully own *all* of this land—agree that justice needs to be served. Together, we will see the vampires of the Vale destroyed."

Most of the wolves in the crowd muttered in agreement, their eyes lit with fire.

"And what of you?" an older male wolf asked from the front, his loud voice booming over the muttered agreements. "If you help us, we will not harm you, but once the vampires of the Vale are destroyed you'll also need to leave our land. Where will you go?"

"The Haven," I said the only answer that made sense. "They'll take in any vampire who's willing to adapt to their ways. They'll provide me safety once this is all over."

"Why not go to the Haven now?" he asked. "Why help your enemy?"

"Because you're not my enemy." I leveled my gaze with his and pointed in the direction of the palace. "*They're* my enemy. They can't continue taking innocent lives like they took mine. They must be stopped. And I'm going to help you stop them."

The crowd burst into applause, and I could tell that I had them.

"Well done," Noah murmured, softly enough so only I could hear.

He took my hand, raised it in the air, and the crowd cheered louder.

"Lady Daria is here to help us!" he yelled, and the crowd quieted at his words. "As I said, she's the vampire spoken of in our dreams. Her help is a sign that our Savior is on His way! Once He rises, it'll be the end of the nomadic, warring life we've been forced to endure for centuries. Once He rises, we'll live in peace and comfort on this land that's rightfully ours! We'll finally have the freedom we deserve!"

The crowd started cheering and clapping again, so enthusiastically that it seemed like they would never stop.

But they *did* stop—when a group of about ten shifters in human form approached the camp.

The men standing around the edges of the crowd shifted into their wolf forms and bared their teeth at the intruders, ready for a fight.

10

KARINA

Noah thrust the scent concealment charm back into my hand.

I placed it around my neck, understanding his intent. Whoever these wolves were, they couldn't know I was a vampire.

Noah had control of his own followers, but he couldn't stop these strangers from attacking me. The concealment charm would keep me safe.

However, by now I had a feeling that the wolves at camp would do whatever was necessary to keep me safe as well—even if it came at the expense of their own lives.

"We come in peace." The leader of the outside pack—at least I *assumed* he was the leader because he was the largest and stood in front of the others—raised his hand in what I assumed meant peace. "Is this the camp of the First Prophet?"

"It is." Noah stepped down from the table and walked through the crowd to face the outside pack's leader. "I am he."

"I am Jakob, and this is my pack." Jakob held out his hand, and Noah shook it. "We heard rumors of wolves throughout the land receiving prophetic dreams that spoke of a Savior, but we didn't believe it until my daughter, Leah, received one herself. Once she told me of her dream, we came to you immediately."

Marigold was instantly at Noah's side. "Which one of you is Leah?" she asked.

"I am." A girl who looked no older than fifteen stepped forward. Her voice was soft, and she kept her eyes focused on the ground, playing with her hands in front of her. "You must be the witch mentioned in my dream."

"I am." Marigold smiled and took Leah's hand, giving the girl a warm smile. "You must be very special to have received a dream from our Savior. What, exactly, did you see?"

"I saw our Savior," she said, her voice so quiet that without my strong vampire senses, I wouldn't have been able to hear her. "He was a wolf more than twice the size of my father—the largest wolf I've ever seen. He said that the time was coming for the wolves in the Vale to reclaim our land. He said that with the help of a witch and a vampire, we would clear the Vale of the vampires, so that He can rise. He promised that once He rose, he would bring peace and prosperity to our packs. And He said that I *must* tell our pack to come here—to this camp—so we could contribute to the cause."

"She's not the only one in our pack to have had the dream." A tall, wiry boy stepped up to join her. "I had the dream too—a few nights ago."

"Then it sounds like you're also very special." Marigold gave him a smile, and he beamed back at her. I had a feeling he didn't receive compliments often. The witch soon turned her attention back to the pack leader. "There's plenty of room for your pack at camp, if you would like to join us," she told him.

"I hope you do," Noah added. "The more of us who band together to fight, the more pleased our Savior will be. He will give His help to all of the wolves of the Vale, of course, but those who fight for Him will be in His best graces."

"Thank you for your kind welcome," Jakob replied. "We'd like to take you up on your offer, and will get ourselves settled in at once."

11

KARINA

Soon after Jakob's pack was shown around they were introduced to me—well, to "Lady Daria." I gave them the same spiel I'd given to the others earlier.

Many wolves came up to greet me individually, some of them offering presents in the form of hand crafted jewelry, pelts, and food. I wouldn't be able to take the gifts back to the palace—not without the vampires becoming suspicious—but I accepted the gifts anyway, grateful for what they symbolized.

The wolves of the Vale trusted me and were welcoming me to their pack.

But I couldn't stay for long, so I soon said my farewells, and Noah escorted me back to the boundary of the vampire kingdom.

"That went well," he told me once we were back.

"It did," I agreed. "Thank you for bringing me there. Seeing the camp…" I paused, contemplating how to express the emotions I felt about the situation. "I never thought I would say this, but you and the other wolves at the camp surprised me. You're good people."

"It only took you until now to realize this?" he asked with a twinkle in his eye.

"Before coming here, I'd never had a conversation with a shifter," I explained. "You must understand that the wolves of the Vale are very different from the wolves that surround the Carpathian Kingdom."

"The wolves near the Carpathian Kingdom have lost touch with their humanity." He said it as a fact, not as a question. "As we had, before receiving our dreams."

"Yes," I answered. "I suppose that must be it."

"Our Savior is a good man." Noah spoke as if he already knew him. "Once He rises, I'm sure He'll want to help shifters all over the world—not just the ones in the Vale. He'll help them get in touch with their humanity once more."

"I hope so," I said, and I meant it. If their Savior could stop the violence around the castle in the Carpathian Kingdom, then all the better.

I just hoped that once He rose, He wouldn't require the sacrifice of any more vampires.

"You look troubled." Noah stepped closer to me, and

it was like his eyes were gazing into my soul. "What's wrong?"

"The Savior is requiring the vampires in the Vale be cleared from the land so He can rise." I needed to tread carefully, since Noah admired the Savior so much. "What happens if He wants *all* the vampires in the world dead once He's here?"

"He won't." Noah spoke calmly and surely. "This land—the Vale—has been sacred since the dawn of time. The wolves who live here have been protecting it for thousands of years—long before the vampires invaded. From what I know, our numbers were far less back then. When Queen Laila settled here with her army of vampires, she was either going to kill my ancestors or make a deal with them. They told her this land was sacred to our kind and she should find somewhere else to go, but learning that the land was sacred made her want it even more. She thought the magic of the land would bring prosperity to her kingdom. My ancestors weren't strong enough to best her in a war, so they agreed to the peace treaty to ensure our survival. Since then, we've grown our numbers, preparing for the time when we could take our land back. The Savior has come to us and told us that the time is now."

"And the vampires of the Vale refuse to leave voluntarily." I said it as a statement, not a question. Over the past few centuries, the Vale had grown into a thriving vampire kingdom. Queen Laila wouldn't leave without a fight.

But this was my species. I didn't want vampires to die if they didn't have to.

"Have you tried to explain the situation to them so they at least have a choice to leave?" I asked.

"The vampires of the Vale won't listen to us," he told me. "The only chance we have to reclaim our land is war. The Savior has told us this in our dreams. But our Savior is a good man. He's rising to bring peace to the world so the fighting can end. And no other kingdom is built on sacred ground, so he'll have no need to expel the vampires from their homes. Once He rises, He'll bring together the wolves and vampires of the Carpathian Kingdom—not pit them against each other. And He certainly won't call for any unnecessary death."

"Thank you," I said, his assurance easing my worries. When he put it that way, I realized how reckless Queen Laila had been to insist on building her kingdom on ground that was sacred to the shifters. She *had* to have known that doing such a thing would eventually have a consequence.

She'd dug herself—and her kingdom—into this grave centuries ago, when she'd ignored the wolves' warning and claimed this land as her own. I couldn't allow myself to feel guilty for her mistake.

"There's no need to thank me." Noah swallowed, his eyes swirling with emotion as he stared at me, and he took my hands in his. "I will do whatever it takes to make sure no harm comes to you, Princess Karina. You have my word—not just as a shifter or as the First Prophet—but as a man whose respect you have earned."

I nodded, unable to break my gaze from his. He spoke so honestly, and I could feel myself being sucked into his intensity, my heart thudding with every second that passed. The warmth of his hands spread through my body, making me feel safe and protected. It was like there was a magnetic force pulling us closer, until there were only inches between us.

I hadn't felt this way around a man since Peter.

The thought of my one true love snapped me back to reality.

I yanked my hands out of Noah's and stepped back, shaking off whatever effect he had on me. Whatever I was feeling for him was only from the intensity of the moment. I couldn't allow myself to forget my motive for being here. I wasn't doing this for the wolves, for their Savior, or for Noah.

I was doing this so I could get Geneva's ring and get Peter back.

My feelings for Noah were fleeting. There was no need to get myself more involved in this war than necessary.

"The sun is growing stronger," I said stiffly, the excuse coming easily. "I need to go back to the palace so I can heal before sunset."

I turned around and hurried away from him, afraid that he might say something that would convince me to stay.

"Wait," he called, just as I'd stepped through the boundary.

I turned around, unable to ignore him completely, and waited for him to continue.

"Stay off the streets tomorrow," he warned, his eyes fierce. "I can't tell you any more—I wasn't even supposed to tell you that at all. But I trust you and I don't want you to get hurt. So stay in the palace tomorrow, and you'll be safe."

I nodded and turned around, running back toward the palace before he had a chance to stop me again.

12

ANNIKA

I APPROACHED Jacen's quarters wearing jeans, a silk tank top, and chunky black heels. The heels were Geneva's insistence. She thought it was horrible that I was dressing so casual for my date with the prince—she'd already selected a gown for me to wear a few days ago—but once I told her of the chat Jacen and I had in the hall, she had no choice but to keep her lips sealed about her thoughts regarding my attire.

I'd also used my power over the ring to command that she kept her opinions to herself.

"Princess Ana," Jacen greeted me upon my arrival. He was also dressed casually, in jeans and a button down shirt. But despite his casual attire, he commanded the room like a prince.

How had I ever believed he was a fellow human

blood slave? The person I was seeing right now was the *real* Jacen.

The vampire prince who used blood slaves and left them for dead without caring in the slightest.

"Your Highness." I lowered myself into an awkward curtsy, the heel of my shoe banging against the floor, and quickly righted myself.

"There's no need for such formalities in private." He stepped aside, ushering me into his rooms. "Please, call me Jacen."

I nodded, looking around his quarters in awe. I'd thought my accommodations in the palace were nice, but Jacen's rooms put mine to shame. The Turkish rug in the entrance probably cost as much as a car.

But the luxurious furniture in his quarters had nothing on the view. The huge window across the way looked out over the entire kingdom.

Next to the window was a table for two that looked like it had been plucked out of a fancy steakhouse.

I immediately felt underdressed in my casual clothing. It took all of my self-control to stop from asking him if I should go back to my room and change into something more appropriate.

Instead, I wrapped my arms around myself, feeling as out of place as ever.

"The chef has prepared a wonderful menu for

tonight." Jacen smiled and led the way to the table. "Come. Let's get started."

We were midway through the second course—a salad—and the date was going horribly. I had no idea what to say or do. Why had conversing with him come so easily to me as Annika, but I was scrambling for conversation now?

The answer was obvious—because Jacen was constantly trying to ask me questions about the Seventh Kingdom. And I was doing my best to avoid answering.

"You seem enamored by the view," he said after a glance out of the window. "Do you have similar views back at your home?"

"We have great views," I said, since I couldn't make the Seventh Kingdom sound like a dump. "But no two views are ever the same, are they?"

"I take it the Seventh Kingdom isn't in the mountains, then?" he asked.

I stilled, aware of what he was doing. It was what he'd been doing all evening—trying to get information about the Seventh Kingdom.

"I'm afraid I'm not at liberty to say," I told him with what I hoped was a polite smile.

It felt like I'd been repeating a similar statement all night.

I took another bite of my salad, wracking my mind for a fresh conversation in the time it took me to chew. What on Earth would he want to talk about? This stiff, domesticated version of Jacen was so different from the wild, rebellious prince I'd known before.

But I needed to remember that the wild rebelliousness had been an act. The Jacen I was sitting across from right now was the real Jacen.

And the two of us had absolutely nothing in common.

"Did you decorate your rooms yourself?" I grimaced after I spoke and stuffed another piece of lettuce into my mouth. Chewing would stop me from saying anything that sounded even stupider.

"No," he told me, and then he placed down his silverware, looking at me seriously.

My stomach plummeted. Was he going to eliminate me on the spot?

After how terribly this date was going, I wouldn't blame him.

"What?" I finally asked.

"I want to keep you here," he told me, and from the sure way he spoke, I had a feeling that he meant it.

"Why?" I asked. "Because if this date is better than

your dates with the other princesses, then those dates must have been flat out torture."

He laughed, and the tension in the room broke for the first time since I'd arrived. "There she is," he said, his eyes still sparkling with laughter.

"Who?" I halfway expected that another princess had appeared in the room behind me. I turned around to look, but nope. It was still just the two of us.

"The spunky girl I spoke with in the hallway the other day—the one who was brave enough to slip out of her dress in front of the entire vampire court and perform a gymnastics routine in her underwear," he said, and my cheeks heated at the reminder of what I'd done on the first night in the palace. I hadn't had a choice, really—it was that or not performing a talent at all. "I want to get to know you, Ana." He leaned forward, his expression turning serious once more. "But I can't do that if you refuse to open up to me about who you are or where you come from. With the way you're holding back, I'm starting to worry that Queen Laila was right, and that the Seventh Kingdom doesn't exist after all."

I swallowed, trying to formulate an answer—and trying to push aside the emotions swirling within me from the intense way he was looking at me. "The Seventh Kingdom exists," I said, the lie feeling heavy as I spoke it. "But you must understand—my kingdom is secretive. Even my coming here was risky. I can't give you any information about the Seventh Kingdom unless you choose me as your bride."

"Is that your way of bribing me to choose you?" he asked, but I could tell by the way his lips curved up slightly that he was joking.

"Of course not," I said quickly. "I would never do that. I guess I was just hoping you would choose me for me, and not because of my kingdom."

"We're royalty, Ana," he reminded me. "We don't always have the luxury of marrying for love. I'm not at liberty to give you much information, but the Vale is in need of an alliance. I need to make sure that the princess I choose comes from a kingdom that will be an asset to my own. How am I supposed to do that when you'll reveal nothing of the Seventh Kingdom?"

Panic fluttered through my chest. He was right. I'd come here hoping he'd pick me on my personality alone, but I hadn't given any consideration to the fact that there was likely more at play.

Jacen wasn't going to choose me as long as he knew nothing about the Seventh Kingdom. Which meant he wasn't going to choose me at all.

I needed Geneva to help me kill Laila sooner rather than later.

In the meantime, I needed to stay in the competition long enough for her to figure out the details on how we could do that.

"You look sad," Jacen observed. "What's wrong?"

"This is a really tough situation for me," I said, since it was the truth. "I've sworn to keep the secrets of the Seventh Kingdom unless you choose me as your bride. But you won't choose me as your bride unless you know about the Seventh Kingdom. What am I supposed to do?"

"It *is* quite the problem," he agreed. "And we certainly aren't getting any closer to solving it in here."

"We definitely aren't." I laughed, since this date was clearly a total bust.

"How about we get out of here?" he asked.

"What?" I startled, since that was the last thing I'd expected him to say. "And go where?"

"Somewhere out of the palace," he said. "These walls can feel like a prison at times. How about we venture outside and take a tour of the town?"

"Okay," I said. "But under one condition."

"And what's that?" he asked.

"That before we leave, I can return to my quarters to change out of these shoes."

13

JACEN

I WAITED OUTSIDE of Princess Ana's quarters as she changed out of her heels, relieved that she'd agreed to my idea to get out of the palace. The date had been going horribly, which was disappointing, given that I'd expected more of her.

I'd been looking forward to this date since running into her on her way to the library. Because I'd recognized the book she was holding. It was from a popular series—the only way someone wouldn't have heard of it was if they were living under a rock—but it was the same book that had been on Annika's bookshelf when I'd spent time with her in her reading nook in the attic above the Tavern. She'd had a bookmark in it, so I knew she'd been reading it.

I couldn't help but feel like the fact that Annika and

Ana were reading the same book was a sign that I should keep Princess Ana around.

It wasn't long before she opened the door and stepped back out into the hall, wearing flats instead of heels.

"All right." She smiled up at me, looking far more relaxed than she had during dinner. "Are you ready?"

"You look beautiful," I told her, since it was true.

"Thanks." She glanced down at the floor, blushing. "But I'm wearing the same thing as earlier. All I changed were my shoes."

"You looked beautiful then, too," I told her, feeling like an idiot for not telling her so the moment she'd stepped into my quarters.

I'd been so consumed with thinking of ways I could get her to tell me more about the Seventh Kingdom that I hadn't really looked at *her*. But that was all about to change. Because she was right. How was she supposed to trust me with such sensitive information when she barely knew me at all?

"This way," I said, linking my arm in hers and leading her down the hall. "Our chariot awaits."

The "chariot" was an elegant golf cart, since there were

no cars in the Vale. The golf carts were mainly for the witches use, or for when royal vampires wanted to journey to town in a more dignified manner than running.

I also thought Ana would enjoy the golf cart ride—it would give her more of an opportunity to take in the sights of the Vale.

My guard Daniel drove us, and Ana's guard sat in the passenger seat, so Ana and I took the row behind them. We didn't say much as we rode, beyond comments about the scenery. I hoped that once we arrived in town and the guards weren't so nearby, Ana would open up more.

We parked a few streets away from the main square, as I'd requested. If we'd pulled straight up to the square, it would have alerted all the vampires that their prince was in town. They would notice soon—and they would certainly notice Ana, since they'd seen her in the parade —but this would help us blend in for slightly longer than we would have been able to otherwise.

"Would you mind standing as far back as you can?" I requested of Daniel and Ana's guard, Tess.

"As far away as is safe," he replied.

"Thank you," I said, and then I led Ana to the main square.

As always, it was bustling with merchants running their street shops. The square was full of mainly vampires, but a few humans as well, since humans occasionally worked as servants for wealthier vampires. The human blood smelled delicious, but I blocked it out and focused on the scent of the food sold in the shops instead.

Vampires didn't *have* to eat food—we could exist on blood alone—but with our heightened senses, food was a luxury that none of us wanted to give up. And this market was known for having the best selection of food in the Vale. Each shop was themed around a different area of the world, and featured the highest quality of food from the region it represented. The selections were superb—the head chef of the palace came here himself to place orders for the royal kitchen.

Ana slowed as we passed one of the booths, and I noticed her eyeing up the selection of French cheeses. She was a woman of my own taste—I could also never resist the call of cheese, even back when I'd been a human.

"We'll take a taste of each," I told the vendor, handing him a large bill before Ana could refuse. "Keep the change."

"That's not necessary," she said. "There's no way I could eat all of that."

"Who said it was all for you?" I asked with a smile. "It just so happens that cheese is one of my favorite foods, and this is the best cheese you'll find in the Vale." I turned back to the merchant, who was already slicing the cheese and preparing our tasting boards. "Two glasses of wine, as well. The Meursault."

"One glass of wine," Ana said. She turned to me and added, "I don't drink."

"Okay." I nodded. I firmly believed that cheese tasted best with wine, but I wouldn't push someone to drink if they didn't want to.

The merchant arranged the tasting boards and told us about each cheese as we tried them. People watched us as they passed—it hadn't taken long for them to notice their prince and one of the princesses I was courting—but they respected our privacy and made no attempts to interrupt our date.

Ana's eyes lit up as she tried one of the cheeses, and at her excited expression, I was glad we'd come out to town instead of staying in the palace.

"You like it?" I couldn't help but smile at how happy she looked.

"It's delicious," she said once she'd finished chewing. Then she gazed thoughtfully around the market, making no move to continue on to the next cheese.

"Is something wrong?" I asked her.

"I've just noticed that only the vampires are buying

food—not the humans," she said. "Do you not allow your humans to eat?"

"They eat," I told her, since obviously they ate—how else would they stay alive?

At the same time, I realized that this was the perfect time to get Ana's opinion on the way humans were treated in the Vale. She'd started this topic—not me. And I intended to glean as much information as I possibly could on her opinions regarding the way the humans here were treated.

If she didn't approve of the way they were treated, she might want to help me bring change to the Vale.

"The food in this market is for vampires only," I continued. "Humans are only allowed certain foods."

"Like what?" she asked, her head tilted in curiosity. "Forgive me for saying so, but I imagine it can't be much, seeing as the humans who live here are quite thin."

"No need to apologize," I told her. I wanted to give her my true opinion on what the humans were and weren't allowed to eat, but vampires with excellent senses surrounded us. I couldn't risk anyone overhearing.

I would just have to observe her reactions to what I said and take from it what I could.

"The humans are allowed a basic fare—rice, beans,

boiled chicken, and the like," I told her. "They're given a certain ration each day. It's enough to keep them functioning so they can do their daily tasks, but nothing more."

"And how do you feel about that?" she asked, not reaching for another piece of cheese.

I couldn't be sure, but her pause made it look like she was refusing to eat any more as some kind of stance for the humans.

I leaned closer to her, my lips brushing her cheek, as if giving her a kiss. I could have sworn she shuddered under my touch. "I don't like it either." I kept my voice low enough that only she could hear. "But we can't discuss it here. We will later, in private. I promise."

She nodded, her eyes locked on mine, and I could tell she was going to hold me to my promise. Her expression was fierce, and her lips parted, making me want to lean close to her again and kiss her. I imagined she would taste sweet, like the cheese she'd just been eating. But I held back, unsure if the move would be welcomed.

When I kissed Princess Ana, it would be when I was sure that she wanted it as much as I did.

For now, I was happy to let the tension between us build. It would make it even sweeter once she finally opened up and let me in.

She stepped back and broke my gaze, glancing

around the market. "We should check out some of the other stalls." Her cheeks flushed as she looked around—it seemed like she was trying to look anywhere but at me. "Do you have any particular favorites?"

Before I could answer, an earsplitting scream sounded from the center of the courtyard, and the market erupted into chaos.

14

ANNIKA

PEOPLE WERE SCREAMING and running out of there. Vampires ran with their enhanced speed, trampling humans in their wake. Everyone's eyes were wide and panicked.

Our guards were by our sides in seconds.

"Run with Princess Ana back to the palace!" Jacen commanded Tess. "It'll be faster than taking the golf cart. Daniel and I will meet you there soon."

Then the prince turned and ran into the chaos, his guard following close behind.

Tess took my arm, but I shook her off, still looking at where Jacen had disappeared. I didn't know *what* was happening in the courtyard, but there were humans here—humans I recognized from when I lived in the village. I couldn't run away without trying to help.

"We have to go back to the palace," Tess said. "The prince commanded it."

I ignored my guard and helped up a human girl who had fallen, stopping her from being trampled. The girl's arm hung at a strange angle—it was clearly broken.

I didn't recognize her, but she looked around the same age as the youngest girl who worked at the Tavern, Martha. I wished I could give her my blood to help her heal. But I wasn't actually a vampire. My blood might not help her like actual vampire blood would. If I tried and it failed—which I suspected it would—I would blow my cover.

"Are you okay to run back to the village?" I asked, looking her over. Her face was smudged with dirt, but beyond her broken arm, everything else seemed fine.

She nodded, her eyes wide with terror as she gazed around at the vampires speeding around her.

At once, I understood her worry. If she tried to run, she would be trampled again.

I tossed her over my back and ran her to a narrow street at the edge of the square, easily navigating through the panicked vampires. I knew this street—it led straight back to the village. As predicted, it was empty of vampires, who were rushing back to their homes.

I placed her down, and she bolted into the alley. I

only looked away once I saw her turn safely around the corner.

Tess was by my side in an instant, her hand on my arm again. "That was very kind of you," she told me, glancing at where the girl had disappeared down the alley. "But we need to leave. Now."

I didn't budge. "The humans are being trampled to death, and no one cares," I said, motioning to the chaos behind us. I hoped Tess would have *some* empathy for the humans, since like all vampires, she'd once been a human as well. "Are you going to help me help them or what?"

She paused, as if sizing me up. "You're stronger than I originally gave you credit for," she finally said with a nod.

Then she hurried back toward the market—I assumed to help.

I let out a long breath of relief and followed, and we each found a human amidst the chaos. This time I found an older man who had been pushed into a stall by the vampires. I was helping him up when an animal rushed through the crowd—a wolf.

The wolf pounced on a vampire, threw her to the ground, and ripped her head off with its teeth. The surrounding vampires screamed, running faster. Another wolf followed close behind the first, also jumping on the closest vampire and ripping into his neck. By the time he was done, the first wolf had already moved onto its next victim.

None of the vampires were fighting back. They were just running away, screaming.

Where was Jacen? I glanced around the square, but he was nowhere to been seen. Had he been one of the victims of the wolves? My stomach lurched at the thought, and I swallowed down the urge to be sick.

But then I remembered the way Jacen had fought off the wolves when they'd cornered us in the forest—back when he knew I was Annika and he was pretending to help me escape. He might have been lying about a lot, but he'd handled himself against the wolves.

I had to trust that he was handling himself with them now.

In the meantime, I needed to get this human man to safety. I threw him over my back and ran to the side street, dropping him off as I'd done for the young girl.

"I hope the prince chooses you," he said with a bow, and then he turned around, hurrying down the alley.

I looked after him, stunned, before refocusing and hurrying back to the square.

Tess had stopped helping humans and was now fighting one of the wolves. She moved in a blur with her sword, but the wolf also moved quickly, managing to avoid being hit in the heart. But his legs were bleeding, which made me hope he would weaken enough for Tess to get the perfect shot.

The other wolf was continuing to leave a line of beheaded vampires in its wake. I still wanted to help the humans… but that wolf needed to be stopped.

I recalled what I knew of fighting wolves—Mike had killed one using a chair leg, but that wolf had been feeding and unprepared for an attack. When Jacen and I had fought the wolves in the forest, we'd jumped onto a tree and used the branches as weapons. We'd been outnumbered, but vampires could jump higher than wolves, which had given us an advantage.

I didn't have any branches right now… but there were plenty of chairs in the now-abandoned stalls. I ran for the closest one and broke off the legs, creating four wooden spears.

Before I had time to make a jump for the nearest tall building, the wolf was running in my direction.

I did the only thing I could think of—I threw one of the spears at his heart.

He dodged it easily, and it clattered to the ground behind him.

I threw the next one and the next, praying that one would hit, but the wolf dodged one while picking up a headless vampire corpse and using it as a shield. The spear wedged itself in the dead vampire's back.

The wolf ran toward me, and I dropped the final spear, reaching into the hidden pocket of my underwear for Geneva's ring. I didn't want to reveal that I had the ring, but it was that or be killed. I *had* to do this.

But before I could touch the ring, the wolf stopped in its tracks. It was only a few feet away, and it stared at me, tilting its head in confusion as it inhaled deeply.

My scent.

I'd learned in the forest that wolves had a stronger sense of smell than vampires. When a human drank the blood of a vampire, they smelled like a vampire to other vampires... but wolves could smell past the deception. The wolves in the forest had known I was a human, even after I'd drank Jacen's blood.

Just like I assumed this wolf could tell I was a human, too.

But why wasn't it attacking? Wolves loved human meat—Mike had been able to kill the wolf that had broken through the boundary a few weeks ago because that wolf had been so consumed with its meal that it hadn't been prepared for an attack.

This wolf was ignoring the humans in the square. It made no sense.

Suddenly, a spear exited the wolves chest—right

where its heart would be—and the wolf toppled to the ground.

Jacen was by my side in an instant. He gripped my arms, as if making sure I was solid and real. "I told you to go back to the palace with Tess!" he said, his eyes swirling with anger.

At the mention of my guard, I glanced over at her—just in time to see her run her blade through the other wolf's heart.

"Is that all of them?" I asked Jacen, breathless as I spoke. "The wolves?"

"They're all dead," he told me. "We killed them."

"Good." I glanced around to check on Tess, spotting her nearby helping more humans. Jacen's guard was nowhere to be found. "Where's Daniel?" I asked him.

"He didn't make it." His eyes went hard, and he glared at the fallen wolf behind me.

"I'm so sorry," I said.

But I wasn't sorry that Daniel was dead.

I was sorry because I'd wanted to be the one to kill him. I'd wanted him to know that the scared human he'd kidnapped over a year ago after killing her family in front of her eyes had finally gotten her revenge.

"You never answered my question." Jacen changed the subject, his hands still on my shoulders, and he was completely focused on me. "Why didn't you return to the palace? As far as I know—which isn't much, given that you've barely told me anything about yourself—you don't have any combat training. You could have been killed."

"There were too many people who needed help," I told him. "The vampires didn't even try to fight—they were all running away. And the humans were helpless in the stampede. They were being trampled—some of them to death. I couldn't just leave them there to die."

"You stayed to help the humans?" He watched me closely, almost as if he were mystified by what I was telling him.

"No one else was helping them," I told him. "I had to do what I could."

His gaze didn't break with mine, and he was watching me so intensely that I nearly forgot to breathe. I couldn't move, I couldn't think—all I could see was the complete admiration in his shining silver eyes.

"What?" I asked shyly. "Why are you looking at me like—"

I was cut off by him leaning down and pressing his lips to mine. The entire market disappeared around me —all that mattered was that Jacen was kissing me, and I was kissing him back.

It had happened so quickly—just like our first kiss in the alley behind the Tavern.

My heart leaped, and I lost myself in his touch. It was like I was myself again—Annika—and I was kissing the prince who I thought was fighting on my side.

I didn't *want* to enjoy kissing him. This was the man who had betrayed me and left me for dead. He didn't care about me or any of the other humans.

But if he didn't care about the humans, why had my desire to help them had such an effect on him? He should have scolded me for helping humans—not kissed me.

What was the prince hiding?

I could have kissed him forever. But just as quickly as the kiss had started, it ended.

I gazed up at Jacen, surprised to see that he looked at breathless as I felt. "What was that for?" I managed to ask, my voice quieter and raspier than usual.

"Do I need to have a reason to kiss you?" He smirked, focusing on my lips.

"No." I straightened, trying to get ahold of myself. "Of course not. It was just unexpected, that's all."

"You impressed me, Ana," he answered, seriously now. "That was the best way to show you how much."

Memories of the kiss we'd just shared flashed through my mind, and it took all of my will power to not lean in and kiss him again. "I didn't realize you cared so much about the humans," I said, pushing my desires away.

I couldn't let one kiss—one *incredible* kiss—distract me from why I was here.

"There's a lot about me you don't know." His eyes flashed with pain, and he glanced around the market, taking in the destruction surrounding us. "And apparently there's a lot about you that I don't know, too," he said, refocusing on me. "I hope that will change, but I'm afraid we're going to have to cut our date short. Because given the events that just occurred, I need to return to the palace and speak with the queen."

15

ANNIKA

"You don't have to walk me to my room," I told Jacen once we made it back to the palace. We both looked a wreck—our clothes and faces were covered in dirt and blood.

Everyone stared at us as we walked down the hall, but no one dared to ask what had happened.

They would know soon enough.

"Yes, I do." He stared ahead with determination, and I knew arguing any further would be futile. Once we reached my door, he placed his hands on my shoulders, looking down at me with fierce protectiveness. It was the same way he'd looked at me when he'd helped escape the Vale—when he knew I was Annika. "We don't know if there are any more wolves inside the boundary," he said, his voice low and serious. "I'm going to assign extra guards to look over you, but I want you to promise me you'll stay in your quarters—where you'll be protected—until I know it's safe."

I pressed my lips together, not liking the thought of being confined to my quarters.

"Please, Ana," he begged. "I of all people understand how frustrating it is to be required to stay in your quarters. But it won't be for long, and I won't be able to focus on weeding out the wolves if I don't know you're safe. If you won't do this for yourself, then do this for me?"

"Fine," I said, since I had a feeling that he meant every word. I was also glad he wasn't asking me to leave the Vale entirely. "But only if you'll give me special permission to check non-fiction books out of the library," I added. "Well, if you'll allow the guards to bring them to me, since I'll be in my quarters."

After all, I couldn't let my time go to waste. If I was stuck in my room, I wanted to use the time to learn as much about supernaturals and the Vale as possible. Hopefully I would find *something* that would give me a clue about how to defeat Laila.

"I thought you preferred fiction?" he asked, smiling for the first time since the attack in the square.

"I do," I said. "But ever since a certain prince so wisely told me the benefits of widening my horizons by reading non-fiction as well, I've been trying to heed his advice."

"This prince does sound quite wise…" he agreed with a smirk.

"You agree then?" I asked.

"Yes," he said. "I agree."

He gave me a quick kiss—too short, compared to the one we'd shared in the square—and then he headed to the queen's quarters, leaving me in my room.

16

ANNIKA

"You could have been killed!" Geneva said after I told her what had happened with the wolves. She'd put up a sound barrier, of course—we couldn't risk any of the guards outside overhearing our conversation. "The prince was right—you should have run back to the palace immediately after the trouble began. It's not just your life you gambled with today—it was mine, too. If you die while in command of my ring, I'll be trapped in it forever. Remember?"

"How could I forget?" I asked, since it was the only reason I trusted Geneva at all. "But right now, I need to shower. Can we finish this conversation once I'm cleaned up?"

"Fine." She huffed and plopped down on my bed. "You do smell revolting. I'll be here when you get out."

I hurried into the shower, taking my time under the flowing water to think over everything that had happened with Jacen and me today. So much had changed… and I had no idea what to think of him anymore. Was he the monster who had tricked me when I'd been a human and had planned on eventually leaving me for dead? Or was he the prince who had looked at me in awe after learning I'd risked my life to save humans during the attack?

Something wasn't adding up. And now, more than ever, I was determined to find out what.

"Took you long enough," Geneva said once I emerged.

I put on my pajamas and sat down on the bed across from her. "Jacen doesn't care about humans," I said what I'd been thinking while in the shower. "He made that clear enough when he said he'd planned on eventually draining me dry. But when I told him that I stayed behind to save human lives today, he kissed me. And I can't for the life of me figure out why."

"It's not *that* difficult to figure out." Geneva smirked. "He's clearly trying to get some nookie."

"What?" I asked, since I had no idea what she meant.

"Sex," she said loudly, rolling her eyes. "Have you considered that he's trying to loosen you up so you'll jump into bed with him?"

"You think he's pretending to care about human lives so I'll hook up with him?"

"I assume that 'hook up' is the new term for nookie?" she asked, and I nodded. "Then yes," she continued. "That's precisely what I think. He *is* a man, after all. Don't let yourself forget that."

"Trust me, I won't." My stomach fluttered at the memory of our kiss once more. "I suppose that might be what he's doing, although from what Eve said in the library, he's already getting that from her." I couldn't keep the disgust from my voice when I said Eve's name. "There's something more he wants from me."

"Pray tell." Geneva leaned forward, clearly ready for gossip.

"He wants information about the Seventh Kingdom," I said, looking her dead in the eye. "He told me that he wants to get to know me better and keep me in the competition, but that it's going to be difficult for him to do if he knows nothing of my kingdom."

"If it's information he wants, then give him some," she said simply. "Say whatever you need to say to get him to choose you."

"How am I supposed to do that?" I snapped, frustration at this entire situation eating away at my bones. "I can't give him information about a kingdom that doesn't exist."

"Luckily, we have some more time in our hands now that you're confined to your quarters for who knows how long." She scooted closer, bringing her hands together in excitement. "So I suppose we might as well get started."

"With what?" I asked.

"Creating the story of the Seventh Kingdom."

CAMELIA

I WAS READYING myself for bed when someone burst into my quarters.

"Camelia?" Queen Laila's voice echoed through my chambers. "Are you in here?"

"Coming," I called from the bathroom, washing off the facemask I was wearing. It was the latest trend I was testing out from the mortal world. It was supposed to have "age-defying" properties, but it hadn't done anything to lessen the wrinkles on my forehead.

I stared angrily at my reflection. I was only twenty-four years old. What kind of twenty-four year old had *wrinkles*?

One who was being forced to constantly use her magic to shield an entire kingdom. At this rate, I would be old and bedridden by the time I was in my forties—just like my mother.

I grabbed my nightcap—a glass of scotch—from the counter and took a sip. The vampires mostly liked wine, but I preferred the hard stuff. I'd been drinking twice the amount as usual since learning that the best way to locate Geneva's sapphire ring would be to make a deal with the fae.

If I retrieved the sapphire ring, Laila would finally give me what I wanted—immortality. She would turn me into a vampire and I would be a princess of the Vale.

I wanted immortality more than anything. But the fae didn't make deals lightly. Whatever they asked of me would surely be something I didn't want to give. And once I called upon them, I would be bound to give them *something*.

But now wasn't the time to stand around worrying, so I forced a pleasant expression on my face and walked out to see what Laila wanted. It was late for her to come by, so whatever it was must be important.

I'd expected to find her sitting on the couch in my living room—Laila never failed to make herself at home when she stopped by—but she was pacing around, her forehead pinched in thought. She didn't even notice when I stepped in.

"Your Highness," I said, making myself known.

"Camelia." She glanced up and stopped pacing. "Finally."

"Would you like me to get you a glass of wine?" I motioned to my small bar.

"No, thank you," she said. "I need my head clear. Come. Let's sit."

I made my way to the sofa, waiting to sit until she was seated first. I was still clueless as to what this could be about, and I took another sip of my scotch, bracing myself for anything.

"The wolves have attacked the town." Her voice was clipped, her eyes hard as she looked at me—as if she was studying me. "This attack is unlike anything we've seen before. It was coordinated. Five of them slipped through the boundary, and together, they orchestrated a terror attack upon the market at its peak hour."

"That's impossible." I gasped. "After the last attack, I strengthened the boundary—it's been taking more magic than I should expend, but I've been doing it. There's no way the wolves could have gotten through."

"There must be a way, because they *did* get through," she said, and from her determined stare, I could tell she wasn't going to budge until she got to the bottom of this. "The only explanation I can think of is that you let them in, so if there's *any* other possible way this could have happened, I advise you tell me now."

Blood drained from my face at the realization that this wasn't just a brief—it was an inquisition.

"There is one possible way." I took a sip of scotch in attempt to calm myself, but it did little for my nerves. "As you know, the barrier only works one way—it keeps people from getting in, but it doesn't keep them from getting out."

"Yes." Laila nodded. "Centuries ago, when the Vale was just starting, your ancestor created a boundary that went both ways. The vampires wouldn't have it. They said I was keeping them prisoner, and we nearly had a revolt. Making it so the boundary didn't keep them in was the only way to placate their fears and keep them happy. The only citizens we needed to keep inside the boundary were the humans, and the threat of the wolves was enough to stop them from escaping."

"I understand," I told her, since I already knew the reason why the boundary was as it was. "This boundary is strong. And while it's extremely difficult to penetrate unnoticed, it's possible. It would involve a witch—a strong witch—and someone who lives inside the boundary working together with the wolves. And five wolves wouldn't have been able to come through at once without my noticing, so they must have come through one at a time."

"Is there a strong enough witch in the palace to pull off such a task?" Laila asked.

"No," I told her, since I was by far the strongest witch here. None of the others compared to me—they wouldn't have stood a chance against my magic. "At least, not one employed by the Vale."

"There's only one witch inside the Vale who's not employed by the Vale." Laila blinked as she put it all together. "Princess Ana's lady's maid."

18

CAMELIA

"You think Princess Ana is working with the wolves?" I balked at the notion of a vampire working with the wolves. Yes, we all suspected that the princess of the supposed "Seventh Kingdom" was up to something, but working with the wolves? Those creatures were far too animalistic to follow through with such an arrangement.

"*One* of the princesses must be," Laila said. "Princess Ana is the only one with a witch strong enough to break through the barrier, and her background is a blatant lie. All I need to do now is increase her security and catch her in the act."

"A solid plan." I nodded, since it was. "But there's one big thing that's not adding up."

"What's that?" Laila asked.

"The wolves that attacked before this were only able

to attack the human village, because humans have no way of smelling the difference between a wolf and anyone else," I started. "But these wolves made it unnoticed to the vampire town until shifting forms. How were they able to do that without any vampires picking up on their scent and reporting them to the guards immediately?"

Laila pulled something out of her pocket—a cloth with something wrapped inside, that sort of looked like an ancient teabag—and tossed it onto the table between us. "Recognize this?" she asked.

I picked it up and studied it, even though I'd felt the aura of dark magic around it instantly. I'd read about dark magic—knowledge was power—but I'd never performed it. Dark magic spells were stronger than natural magic, but they required the blood of someone slain by the caster's hand to work. Using it was addicting. A witch who performed dark magic lost some of his or her natural ability to perform magic with each spell cast, until they were reliant on dark magic and dark magic alone for the rest of their lives.

"It's a chameleon charm," I said. "Created with dark magic so it can hide supernaturals."

Such charms could be created with regular magic to hide humans from supernaturals, but creating one to hide supernaturals from supernaturals was another beast entirely. Thus why it required dark magic.

"I suspected as much," Laila said. "Ana's guard Tess took it off a wolf she killed. It's further evidence that the wolves are being helped by a witch."

"Princess Ana was there during the attack?" I asked. Surely that made her *and* her witch look guilty.

"She was on a date with Jacen—the two of them went to the market," Laila said. "His idea, apparently. If Jacen and the guards hadn't been there, the attack would have been much worse than it was."

"I should go to the attack site," I told her. "See if I can find any more clues."

"You'll do no such thing." Laila's voice was sharp, and I sat back in surprise. "Until we find proof that Princess Ana is working with the wolves, you're still one of the suspects. You'll remain in your quarters until this problem is resolved."

"You're putting me under house arrest?" I looked at her, stunned. I already wasn't permitted to leave the Vale, since they needed me here to maintain the boundary. Now she was keeping me in my *quarters*?

She raised an eyebrow. "Would you prefer the dungeons?"

"Of course not." I shuddered at the suggestion.

Then I forced myself to get ahold of myself. Because there was still *one* place where I had the upper hand.

"What about when I go to the fae?" I asked.

"I hadn't realized you'd decided to seek out the fae." Laila smiled, clearly pleased with my decision.

"They're the only creatures who will know where Geneva's ring is and how I can get it," I said, since it was true. The fae were more similar to gods than to what mortals traditionally thought of as faeries. They ruled from the Otherworld—rarely ever crossing over to our world—but they knew everything that was happening on Earth. If anyone had the answers I needed, it was the fae. "But I'll only go to them if you make a blood oath with me that you'll turn me into a vampire princess after I hand over the ring."

"Deal," Laila said, and I sat back, surprised by how easy that had been. "Now, you already know you must wait for the full moon for your upcoming journey. Let me tell you exactly what you need to do when the night comes and it's time for you to call upon the fae…"

She gave me the instructions, and once the explanation was complete, we sealed the blood oath.

19

ANNIKA

I'D BEEN in my quarters for nearly three days—the only times the door ever opened was when the guards delivered my meals or books. Geneva and I spent a good amount of the time creating the details of the imaginary Seventh Kingdom. I liked what we'd created—it seemed like we'd thought of something that would be near impossible for Queen Laila to disprove. I still wanted to avoid giving out *too* much information, but at least I now had something to tell Jacen if it seemed like he was considering eliminating me from his selection again.

I hated lying, but it had already gotten me this far. What was one more major lie on top of everything else?

Eventually, someone knocked on the door at a time not designated for meals. I hadn't requested a new round of books, so my breath caught at the possibility that it might be Jacen coming to update me on what was going on in the kingdom.

I glanced in the mirror, quickly running a brush through my hair, and hurried to answer the door.

It wasn't Jacen waiting on the other side—it was Tess.

"Don't look too excited to see me," she joked with a small smile. Ever since we'd worked together in the square to save the humans, the relationship between us had lightened greatly. I trusted Tess, and I was glad she'd been assigned to be my guard.

"Sorry," I said, forcing a smile on my face as well. "I'd just been hoping…" I trailed off, not wanting to say it out loud.

"You were hoping I would be the prince?" she finished my thought.

"Yes." I straightened, pushing the notion away. "But of course I'm happy to see you. Has there been any news since the attack?"

"Nothing I'm at liberty to say," she said *"But* I've been asked to inform you that Prince Jacen requests the presence of all the foreign princesses in the throne room immediately."

"Immediately?" I looked down at my pajamas in horror. I'd been spending most of the day reading and hadn't even showered yet. "Do we at least have five minutes to freshen up?"

"Five minutes," she agreed. "If you're not ready by then, I'll come in there and drag you to the throne room myself."

20

ANNIKA

I was ready quickly enough that no dragging of any sort was necessary.

Tess led me to the throne room, where all the other princesses were already waiting. They all looked perfect and pristine.

Apparently, they'd all been ready to see the prince at a moment's notice.

Jacen sat on the throne, wearing all black. The throne next to him was empty. He was the only royal member of the Vale in the room—both Queen Laila and Camelia were absent.

His gaze locked on mine, and he looked at me as if I were the only other person in the room. It was like time stood still, and I couldn't move, speak, or breathe. All I could do was look right back at him, and I was sure I looked just as star struck as he.

Eventually, he broke his gaze with mine. "Now that everyone's here, we can begin," he said, strong and in command.

I looked around the room once more, surprised that *no* other royals from the Vale were there. So far, Queen Laila had been present at every important moment of Jacen's selection process. There were only two reasons why I could think she wasn't here now. Either this wasn't an important moment, or she had more pressing matters to attend to.

Given the recent attack, I assumed the latter.

"Firstly, I want to thank all of you for coming to the Vale to meet me and be a part of my marriage selection process." Jacen stood up from his throne, and gazed around at each of us. "However, as you're well aware by now, we recently suffered an attack from the wolves that live outside of our boundary. The attack resulted in multiple casualties. The queen has had the kingdom thoroughly investigated, and we've concluded that there are no more wolves within our walls. But we've taken the attack as a declaration of war, and acknowledge that by you all staying in our palace, your lives are at risk."

I swallowed, bracing myself for what was coming next. He was clearly about to hold an elimination. And from the way he was talking, it sounded like he was going to ask us *all* to return home.

If he did that, everything I'd been through since coming to the palace would have been for nothing.

"You're all wonderful women, and I've enjoyed getting to know you," he said. "But by this point, I've had one on one time with each of you and it's become clear which of you I could see myself spending my life with, and which of you I couldn't."

Eve brought her hair over her shoulders and smiled seductively at the prince, clearly confident about which category she fell under.

Jacen barely looked at her, stone cold as he continued. "I have no desire to lead any of you on," he said. "But more so, I have no desire to put you in unnecessary danger. Especially because at this point, there are only two princesses I want to continue to pursue." He paused, and I could barely breathe as I waited for him to name the two. "Princess Karina and Princess Ana."

"What?" Eve shrieked, looking lost and stranded as she pouted up at the prince.

For the first time, I felt sorry for her.

But then I remembered the way she'd cornered me and bullied me in the library, and any sympathy I'd felt for her vanished.

"Princess Karina and Princess Ana are the only two

princesses who will remain in the palace, and thus, they are the only two princesses eligible for my hand in marriage." Jacen stared at Eve as he spoke, and she narrowed her eyes in anger. He looked away from her and continued, "I'll have a date with Princess Karina tomorrow night, and a date with Princess Ana the night after. The rest of you are to return to your quarters, pack your bags, and return to your kingdoms at once."

"The vampires of Utopia are correct about men." Margaret—the other princess from Utopia—took Eve's hand, glaring at Jacen. "You're selfish and cruel to take advantage of my sister the way you did."

"If any of you feel like you were put into any situation while in this kingdom without your consent, please speak now." Jacen was calm as he replied to Margaret, and Eve turned her eyes down, unwilling to look at him. He gave us a few moments to reply. When no one did, he continued, "As I thought. Now, I need to return to strategizing our retaliation against the wolves. I expect all of you except for Princess Karina and Princess Ana to be gone from the Vale by the next sunset."

He left the room via a side door without glancing back at any of us.

I watched him leave, stunned.

This selection process was supposed to have lasted much, much longer. Weeks, or even months. Geneva and I had discussed my *trying* to become Jacen's bride, but I hadn't actually thought he might choose me. I'd thought I would stay in the palace for as long as possible, and during that time Geneva and I would be brainstorming a way to kill Queen Laila undetected before Jacen eliminated me.

Now, for reasons I didn't understand, I had a fifty percent chance of marrying Jacen and becoming a princess of the Vale.

I still wanted Laila dead, but I also couldn't ignore the feeling that something wasn't adding up about Jacen's motives, and that until I could pinpoint exactly what was going on with him, I might not be able to betray him.

21

JACEN

Laila flung my double doors open with so much force that they slammed into the walls behind them.

"*All* of the princesses?!" She barged inside, her hair and dress flying behind her as she stomped toward where I sat at my desk. "You just eliminated *all* of the princesses?!" She banged her fists onto the desk, seething as she stared down at me.

Her guards took the liberty of closing my doors and leaving my room.

"You've heard incorrectly," I said calmly, leaning back into my chair. "I didn't eliminate *all* of the princesses. Karina and Ana still remain."

"Oh, I *did* hear correctly." She sneered. "That pretender Ana was never in the running, and you and I both know that. You will rescind your decision immediately and the other princesses will remain in the palace."

"I will do no such thing," I told her. "A betrayer is in our midst, and the princesses are the main suspects. You've told me yourself that you trust the Carpathian Kingdom, and you agreed with me that Princess Ana was best kept here, where we can keep an eye on her. By eliminating the others, I was sending home potential enemies, and thus, doing the Vale a favor."

"You deliberately overstepped my authority," she said. "I should have had Stephenie make this alliance, not you."

"Except that Stephenie isn't here," I reminded her. "I am. And if Stephenie even managed to stop partying for long enough to get married, she would go live with her husband. With the strength of the wolves rising, we needed to do this now—you had no time to successfully turn another prince and for him to learn to control his bloodlust. I was the only option you had."

"You overstep your place here, Jacen." She zipped around the desk, yanked out a stake that had been strapped to her thigh, and rammed it into my stomach.

I gasped as the pain overtook my body, another crippling wave of it wracking through me as the tip of the weapon scratched my heart. One move forward and I would be dead.

Attempt to fight her and I would surely be dead, too.

"I created you." Laila twisted the stake and smiled, clearly enjoying my grunts of pain. "I can destroy you, too."

"Do it," I dared her, forcing myself to speak through the agony. "It's what you should have done last year when I killed all those humans in the village."

"Oh, I never said I was going to kill you." She yanked out the stake, and I pressed my hands to my stomach as my body started to heal. "There are many, many other ways a person can be destroyed. I've been around for long enough to know these things. Going against me was a mistake, Jacen." She twirled the stake around and licked the tip of it, relishing in the taste of my blood before placing it down on the desk in front of me.

If I wanted to, I could grab it and attack.

But that was what Laila *expected* me to do.

Instead, I lifted the stake and handed it to her. "I didn't go against you," I said, but she just stared at the weapon, not moving toward it. "I promised I wouldn't eliminate Princess Karina without consulting you first, and I stuck to my word. In fact, I plan on proposing to her."

It was a lie, of course. Once I saw Ana risk herself to save those humans during the attack, I knew I was going to choose her. She'd put the lives of a few humans above her own. *She* was the princess I needed by my side to bring true change to the Vale.

I'd also known after kissing her that I was falling in love with her. Her kiss was so familiar... almost as if we'd kissed before.

Kissing her was like coming home.

But Laila was right—I may have grown overly confident on what I could get away with. Once I'd decided on proposing to Princess Ana, keeping the other princesses in the Vale had seemed pointless. I'd meant it when I'd told them I had no desire to keep them in harm's way or to lead them on. I didn't regret my decision. After all, Princess Ana could have been killed during the attack. If the worst happened, and one of the other princesses died on my watch when I could have easily sent them home to safety, I'd have to live with the guilt of their death forever.

I had enough death to live with without adding theirs on top of it.

I should have sent Ana home, too. Wherever the Seventh Kingdom was, she would be safer there than here.

But if I sent her home, I might never see her again. And I couldn't lose her. Not now, when I was just getting to know her.

I also had another reason for wanting to keep her.

Because in the square, the wolf had run at Ana, ready to kill. Then he'd stopped.

The wolves had killed all the other vampires with reckless abandon.

What made Princess Ana so different?

I'd been thinking on it for the past few days, and one answer kept coming to me—she was working with the wolves.

The wolf hadn't attacked her because they were fighting on the same side.

If I could gain her trust and get her to admit that to me, perhaps I could *join* her and the wolves in their war against the Vale. It would be the perfect opportunity to bring down this kingdom once and for all.

But having the queen so livid at me would get me nowhere. And Laila had been pushing me to make an alliance with the Carpathian Kingdom from the get-go. Telling her that I intended to marry Princess Karina struck me as the perfect way to end this fight and convince the queen that I was still under her thumb, just like she wanted.

"You've come to a decision so soon?" Laila reached for the stake and shoved it back into the holster around her thigh, still looking down at me suspiciously.

I stood, since remaining seated while the queen was standing was defiant against her authority. "I have." I nodded. "Princess Karina has opened up to me in a way that none of the other princesses have," I said, since it was the truth. Karina had told me all about her lost love, Peter, even though doing so had made her vulnerable. "I haven't been able to stop thinking about her since we danced on the night of the ball." A lie—I hadn't been able to stop thinking about *Ana* since her gymnastics performance on the night of the ball—but right now, the lie was necessary. "The reason why I so easily agreed to not eliminate Karina without your consent was because by then, I already knew I wanted her."

"So why not say so then?" she asked.

"Because at that point, we'd talked up the competition for my hand so much that the citizens of the Vale would have been disappointed if we hadn't given them the show we'd promised," I said simply. "I saw no point in committing to anything at that point in time. But the recent attack changed everything. We can't risk the other princesses remaining in our kingdom. If any of them were killed while under our protection, it would mean not just war with the wolves, but potential war with their kingdom as well. Best not to ruffle any feathers, don't you agree?"

"I do." She nodded, although she still looked at me like she wasn't convinced. "You would have discovered as much if you hadn't circumvented my authority and had come to me with all of this *before* announcing your decision to the princesses, but that's not important right now. Because there's one big thing that isn't adding up."

"What's that?" I asked.

"Princess Ana," she said. "Why keep her around when you've already decided to propose to Princess Karina?"

"Because she's most likely the one who's been working with the wolves," I said simply. "Why send her away when we can keep her here of her own free will and catch her in the act?"

"You've kept her here so we can spy on her?" Laila arched an eyebrow.

"Yes," I said, although if I found any evidence of her working with the wolves, I was damned well going to cover it up and keep her safe. And if I was going to propose to her—which I fully intended on doing—I needed to prove her innocence. To do that, I needed time. "We couldn't keep her prisoner without evidence, and setting her loose would be foolish. Keeping here her under her own free will seemed the best course of action."

"It is logical," Laila agreed. "But in the future, you'll come to me—your *queen*—before making another major decision like that. I took it easy on you with that stake. It's best you not forget that there are other ways I can break you. For instance, you remember that human blood slave Annika, don't you? How I killed her?"

I nodded, tensing at the mention of Annika. What did she have to do with any of this?

I thought Laila had forgotten about her by now.

"I know you cared about her." She sat down atop my desk and crossed her legs, revealing the bloodied stake strapped to her thigh. "That was why I killed her. If you defy me again, I swear upon the angels themselves that for the rest of your immortal existence, I will destroy everything you ever come to love."

"Understood," I said, although there was only one thing I truly understood—Laila intended to keep me under her thumb for all eternity.

Which gave me only one option.

I needed Princess Ana to trust me enough to introduce me to the wolves she was working with so we could take down the Vale and Queen Laila together.

22

KARINA

My second date with Jacen was a similar setup as the first—a formal, private dinner in his quarters.

"I was hoping to get more creative with our second date," he apologized as he led me to the table. "But after the attack in town, I thought it best that we remain inside the palace."

The attack had been caused by the "scouts" Noah had sent into the boundary. I couldn't help but feel like Noah had lied to me. Marigold, too. They'd known they were sending those young wolves into the boundary for a kamikaze mission—a declaration of war—but they hadn't told me the plan. They'd just had me do my part, and that was it.

But why should I have expected anything more? Yes,

I was helping the wolves, but I was still a vampire. An outsider to the pack.

At least Noah had warned me to stay inside that night. I didn't know what I would have done if I'd been on the streets, as Jacen and Princess Ana had been. I supposed I would have fought. What other choice would I have had? Most everyone knew I was a skilled fighter who had helped defend the Carpathian castle from the wolves in the Great War.

If the vampires of the Vale had cared at all about honing their fighting skills, perhaps so many of them wouldn't have died in the attack. They'd been comfortable and safe for far too long. Only the guards here had any fighting skills, and they only knew how to protect themselves against vampires.

When the full pack of wolves broke through the boundary, it was going to be a bloodbath.

"I thought you and Queen Laila had verified that there were no more wolves in the boundary?" I asked Jacen as I took my seat.

"We have," he said. "But I thought it best to be safe."

"Makes sense," I agreed.

A waiter came inside to pour our wine and serve our first course—a tray of caviar with all the necessary garnishes. I adored caviar, and was quick to dig in.

"How's the town faring since the attack?" I asked Jacen once the waiter left.

Jacen made himself a caviar cracker and popped it into his mouth, waiting to answer until he finished chewing. "Not well," he finally admitted. "They're scared. Understandably so. Some vampires have left to go to the Haven—including some guards who didn't want to be separated from their families."

I sipped my wine, secretly relieved that vampires were opting to leave for the Haven. The fewer vampires remaining in the Vale when the wolves attacked, the better. I might be helping the wolves in this war, but that didn't mean I wanted to see innocent members of my own species slain.

I simply wanted Peter back much, much more.

It wasn't long before we finished the caviar—I'd eaten most of it, as Jacen didn't seem overly fond of it—and moved on to soup.

As we ate, I thought about what Noah had said on our way back from the camp—about how there was no point in attempting to reason with the vampires, since they wouldn't listen. I certainly agreed with him that *Queen Laila* wouldn't listen. But Jacen had only been a vampire for little over a year—he wasn't as tied to this land as Laila was. He'd said he understood why some vampires were leaving from the Haven. Perhaps if Noah reached out to *Jacen* instead of Laila…

"Do you have any idea why the wolves are attacking?" I asked, since it would be unwise to ask the prince straight off the bat if he'd considered reaching out to them himself.

"It's about land," he told me. "They see how we turned our land from empty wilderness to a prosperous kingdom, and they're jealous."

"But Queen Laila made a peace treaty with them when she settled here," I said, since the treaty was common knowledge. "They signed it willingly."

"Centuries ago," he said. "Now, the wolves are jealous of our kingdom, and they want this land back."

"But why would they choose *now* to wage war?" It was a question I would have thought whether I knew the wolves' motives or not. "There has to be a deeper reason."

"If there is, we'll likely never know." He shrugged and pushed away his soup, apparently finished. "The wolves are killers. *Monsters*. They're not capable of rational thought. You know this—your castle in the Carpathian Kingdom is surrounded by wolves as well, right?"

"It is." I nodded.

"Then you must know what they're like when they attack." He sat straighter, his eyes full of fire. "They tore into vampires' necks like it was nothing, ripping their heads from their bodies like rag dolls. We're lucky that we stopped them when we did. If I hadn't been there with Princess Ana and our guards, there would have been many more casualties."

"I heard you fought the wolves bravely," I said, assuming that Jacen—like most people—would appreciate the compliment.

"I did my best," he replied. "After I was turned, the queen wouldn't let me leave the palace until I gained control over my bloodlust. Without the Olympics to train for anymore, I needed *something* to focus on. I figured that combat would be a logical choice. The guards were more than happy to give me lessons."

"It seems they've taught you well," I said.

"They have," he agreed. "Although I'm of course still learning."

"Of course," I said. It was clear how Jacen had qualified for the Olympics as a human—he wasn't the type to stop training until he was the best.

The waiters cleared our plates and brought out the third course—salad. I'd never liked salad much, unless it was Caesar salad, which this one wasn't. I would likely pick at it until the main course arrived.

"I agree that the wolves likely don't want to talk," I

said, waiting once more for the waiters to leave. "But for curiosity's sake, let's say they did."

"They don't." He jabbed his fork into his salad. "What use is it pretending otherwise?"

"Your time as prince of the Vale is only just beginning," I told him. "You have many more challenges ahead of you. Since there's a chance we might be… working together in the future, I thought it might be fun to discuss hypothetical situations. Unless, of course, that's not the type of relationship you want from your future bride?"

He chewed, his brow creased in thought. The prince truly was handsome. When I was a young girl—before meeting Peter—I surely would have been smitten with him.

"It *is* the type of relationship I want with my future bride," he said after he swallowed his food. "My answer is yes. If the wolves wanted to have a civil discussion, I would be open to hearing them out. I'm not sure what agreement could be reached—not after they've killed so many vampires—but I don't want any more blood spilled than necessary."

"Very sensible," I said, pushing the lettuce around on my plate to make it look like I'd eaten more than I had. "Not like it matters, of course, since the wolves are monsters." I needed to make sure he believed I thought that. Queen Laila didn't suspect that I was the traitor—the Carpathian Kingdom had a fantastic, long-standing relationship with the Vale—but I couldn't risk saying anything that might tip Jacen off.

However, I was glad he would be open to a meeting with the wolves. Perhaps, if that happened, I could convince Noah to make a deal with Jacen that would spare the prince's life. Jacen might even try to convince as many of the Vale's vampires as possible to leave for the Haven at once.

"That they are," he agreed, and then he glanced at my plate. "Is there something wrong with your salad?"

"Not at all," I said, and then I leaned forward, as if about to tell him a juicy secret. "Although I suppose I must admit I've never been particularly fond of salad."

"I could take it or leave it." He shrugged. "Onto the next course then?"

"Onto the next course," I agreed, and he called the waiters in.

Our salads were soon replaced with sizzling steaks—cooked rare, of course. I'd yet to meet a vampire that didn't love red meat. My mouth watered at the delicious smell, and I quickly dug in.

"I don't think I've had the opportunity yet to thank you," I told Jacen, feeling like it was time to steer the conversation away from the wolves.

"For what?" he asked.

"For keeping me here." I chuckled, since I'd thought it had been obvious. "Eliminating everyone but myself and Princess Ana was a bold move, and while I don't know what I did that compelled you to want to keep me here, I'm glad you did."

"I like you, Karina." His eyes were full of honesty, and my stomach twisted with the knowledge of how I was deceiving him. "The time we've spent together has been... educational. There's depth to your soul, and not only do I admire that, but I'm grateful that you've opened up to me and let me see you for who you are. You would bring much to the table as a princess of the Vale."

I forced myself to smile as he spoke, grateful that he didn't bring up love. Because it *did* seem like Jacen respected me. Perhaps he even thought we could grow to fall in love with each other.

But if he chose me, he would clearly be making a political decision—not a romantic one.

It wasn't supposed to have gotten this far. This selection process was supposed to have taken weeks. Now, it was down to me and that strange imposter Ana.

If the Vale was looking for an alliance—which they clearly were—they would be foolish to form one with a kingdom they knew nothing about. The only reason

Queen Laila would want to keep Princess Ana around would be to learn more about the so-called Seventh Kingdom. Once she had proof that the Seventh Kingdom was fake—which we all knew it was—I would be the only princess left.

Which meant Jacen had already chosen me. After Queen Laila uncovered the truth about Princess Ana, the engagement would become official.

I didn't want to be married to someone else when Peter returned to me. I couldn't have a weight like that between us.

There was only one solution—I needed to go to Noah and ensure that the wolves launched their full attack *before* the wedding—or at least before Jacen and I had the chance to say "I do."

23

KARINA

I RETURNED to my quarters wracked with guilt.

"How did your date go with the prince?" my lady's maid, Elena, asked as she emerged from her room. She was the closest person I had to a friend back in the Carpathian Kingdom. But now that I was keeping so many secrets—mainly, now that I was working with the wolves—I felt more distant from her than ever.

"Very well." I forced a smile. "I believe Prince Jacen intends on proposing to me."

"That's incredible!" Elena gushed. "Do you have any idea when? He needs to eliminate the imposter princess first, right?"

In private, that was how we referred to Ana—as the imposter princess. We would never dare say it in public, of course, but most everyone suspected that Ana was a liar. Only foolish idealists believed the Seventh Kingdom existed.

"He does," I confirmed. "But please, leave me." I paused, looking her in the eye and injecting magic into my tone. "Return to your room, close the door, and go to sleep. Don't come out until the sun sets."

Her face slacked as she responded to the compulsion, and she did as I commanded.

Once she was gone, I collapsed onto my bed and stared up at the canopy overhead. All of those vampires who were killed during the attack... their deaths were *my* fault. If I hadn't helped the wolves, they would still be alive.

I removed my portrait of Peter from under my pillow and stared at it, needing to remind myself why I was doing this. I remembered exactly when he'd had the portrait taken—on the transatlantic voyage we'd taken on the *Olympic*. I'd met him on deck as the ship had left port—he'd been a human, and I a vampire—and we'd spent the entire journey together. We hadn't been sure we would see each other again after the voyage, and he'd given the portrait to me, so I'd always remember him.

He'd ended up proposing on the final night of the voyage. When I'd told him I was a vampire, he came with me to the Carpathian Kingdom, where we received permission from King Nicolae for me to turn him. I had many other pictures of Peter, of course, but this one meant the world to me because it was the first thing he'd ever given me.

Peter had been murdered by wolves inside our own home during the Great War. The Nephilim had sent the wolves into the castle first to weaken us before their attack. Yes, we'd ended up defeating the Nephilim, but Peter's life—and the lives of so many others—had been cut off too short because of that war.

I'd always blamed the wolves for his death. But after what Noah had told me—how those wolves had lost touch with their humanity—I realized that it wasn't the wolves' fault. It was the Nephilim. It was, after all, the Nephilim who had controlled the wolves.

As I stared into Peter's eyes, I imagined how incredible it would be to have him with me again—*alive*—instead of only seeing him in photographs.

I was so, so close to getting what I wanted. The attack had proven that the vampires of the Vale were weak after decades of peace. Once the wolves fought them for real, the Vale would be demolished. Once the Vale was demolished and King Nicolae took Laila back to the Carpathian Kingdom, he was bound by the blood oath to get me Geneva's sapphire ring.

I'd thought I could live with all of that death on my

hands—I'd thought it would be worth it to be reunited with Peter.

But I now knew that vampires were voluntarily leaving the Vale for the Haven. Queen Laila would never abandon the Vale—I knew that. But Noah had seemed so convinced that *none* of the vampires of the Vale would leave voluntarily.

The fact that some of them had proved him wrong.

If there was a way to save as many lives as I could and still get Peter back, I needed to try. The sun had risen and the vampires were asleep. It was the perfect time to speak with Noah.

And so, I changed—placing the portrait of Peter deep in my jacket pocket—texted Noah with a meeting spot, and left through my window.

24

KARINA

As always, I met Noah on the edge of the boundary—me remaining inside, and him remaining out.

"You appear in good health." He smiled when he saw me. "I assume you heeded my warning?"

"I did," I replied. "Thank you for the heads up."

I wanted to add something about how I could have held my own if I'd been out on the streets during the attack, but I held my tongue. Because would I have been able to fight those young wolves who I'd helped sneak through the boundary? I didn't think so. So yes, I *was* grateful for Noah's warning. It had ensured that I hadn't found myself in an even stickier situation than I was in right now.

"I didn't think I would be seeing you again so soon." Noah looked at me in concern. "Is everything all right?"

I wanted to dig into him and tell him that he should have told me that the wolves were being sent into the boundary not as scouts, but to launch an attack, but I held my tongue once more. Because I wanted something from Noah. Putting him on the defensive was hardly the way to get what I wanted.

"Prince Jacen eliminated all the princesses but myself and one other," I told him instead.

"Because of the attacks?" he asked.

"Yes," I said. "He didn't want to risk any of the princesses getting hurt in the chance of another attack."

"I'm grateful that the prince kept you." Noah stepped forward, close enough that he was nearly brushing up against the boundary. "I must say—I can't fault him for his taste."

"Thank you." Heat rose to my cheeks at the compliment, and I inwardly cursed at myself for blushing.

"Which other princess did he keep?" he asked.

"The imposter princess," I told him. "The one from the 'Seventh Kingdom.' I have a feeling that Jacen's waiting for Queen Laila to get proof that she's a fake, and then he's going to propose to me."

"You don't sound too happy about it," Noah observed.

"I'm not," I said. "You were supposed to have completed your mission *before* the prince chose a bride."

"You can't go blaming us about this." Noah held his hands up and took a step back. "We had no control over the prince sending home so many princesses at once. It's as unexpected to me as it was to you."

"I know that." I huffed, since it was pointless to take out my irritation on Noah. Jacen's decision wasn't *Noah's* fault. No one could have predicted that the prince would have been so… noble. "But it's what has happened. Anyway, I'm here for an entirely different matter."

"And what's that?" he asked. "You've done so much to help me that if there's anything you need, just ask. I'll do whatever I can to make it happen."

"I'd like for you to speak with Prince Jacen," I told him.

"What?" He balked.

"You heard me." I held my ground, wanting him to know I was serious. "I've been spending time alone with the prince, and I believe he would be interested in hearing what you have to say. He doesn't want people to die. I don't either—and I would hope that you agree. If there's a way for you and Prince Jacen of you to work together to save lives while still allowing your Savior to rise… I think you should try."

"Except that there *is* no compromise that can be made," Noah insisted. "The vampires of the Vale must be cleared from the land for our Savior to rise. You know that, Karina. There's no other option."

"What if Prince Jacen led the vampires of the Vale to a new location?" I asked.

"Queen Laila would never allow it," Noah said. "She loves this land. It's been her home for centuries. But even more so—she loves it *because* it's sacred. She's not going to give it up."

"I wasn't speaking about Queen Laila," I said, since he was right—the queen wouldn't give up her land without a fight. "I was speaking about Prince Jacen."

"You think the prince will go against his queen?" Noah raised an eyebrow, clearly already sure of the answer to the question.

"Perhaps," I said. "He was turned into a vampire against his will, and from what he's told me, he's *not* happy about it. He hates how Laila doesn't give humans a choice on being turned or not. I believe Prince Jacen would be open to breaking from Queen Laila and starting his own kingdom, if he were presented with the option."

"Let's say I was willing to speak with the prince," Noah said. "And that's a big if. What would stop him from bringing his guards and attacking then and there?"

"A valid concern," I said. "But this is why we have the Haven. Reach out to them with your plan, and they will send witch envoys to transport you and Jacen to a safe location where you can talk."

"The Haven would involve themselves in politics?" he asked.

"They wouldn't technically be involving themselves," I explained. "They would be providing a safe space for two leaders about to go to war to talk so they can *prevent* war. Situations like this one are precisely why a neutral kingdom like the Haven is necessary. You'll both be granted safety while in the Haven, and will be able to talk without worrying about any threats."

"And if the prince tries to attack me once we're there anyway?" he asked.

"He won't," I assured him. "It's against the law to wage war—or cause any type of violence—on the grounds of the Haven. If he does try anything, he'll surely see the wrath of the Haven's tiger shifters."

Noah's forehead crinkled—I had a feeling he was giving my suggestion true consideration. "I'll think about it," he finally said. "I'm not a killer, and neither is our Savior. We're eager for Him to rise because we want peace. If there's a way to spare lives—even vampire lives —then I owe it to Him to try."

"Thank you." I let out a long breath, glad that Noah was seeing reason.

If it hadn't been for the barrier between us, I might have even hugged him.

"Is that the only reason you wanted to speak with me, princess?" From the way he was watching me, I could tell he was hoping for something more.

"There is one more request I'd like to make," I started.

"Go on." He looked at me to continue.

"I'd like for you to ensure that the wolves launch their attack *before* my wedding to the prince."

He smiled—apparently he liked my request. "I'd also like for you to remain unmarried," he said, fire sparking in his unwavering gaze.

My heart raced so intensely that I was inclined to take a step back.

"I'll do what I can," he continued. "But it's imperative that we attack when the time is right. If that time is after the wedding… then I must do what's best for the pack. I hope you understand."

"I do." I nodded—it looked like I would have to figure out how to delay the wedding on my own. "In the meantime, please keep me posted on how the conversation goes with Prince Jacen, if you decide to speak with him at all."

"That," he said with a smile, "Is certainly a promise I can keep."

25

ANNIKA

I was so nervous for my date with Jacen that I felt like I was going to be sick.

It had been days since our kiss in the town—and the kiss had happened so quickly, so in the heat of the moment, that I couldn't be sure if it meant anything to the prince at all.

The worst was that I *wanted* it to mean something to him... because it had meant something to me. I knew it shouldn't—that the prince was a cold-hearted liar—but I couldn't forget how impressed he'd looked by my desire to help the humans during the attack.

Surely someone who didn't care about humans would have thought that my risking my life for theirs was foolish?

I also didn't understand why he'd eliminated all of the princesses except for me and Princess Karina.

Prince Jacen was a puzzle that I couldn't figure out, and my inability to piece him together was driving me crazy.

As I prepared for the date, I took steady breaths, reminding myself that I needed to get my head in the game. I was here to destroy the queen—I couldn't let myself forget that.

Geneva coerced me into wearing a dress. It was green and short, which was good because I wouldn't risk tripping on it. I couldn't deny that the green looked good against the long red hair of the girl I was masquerading as. Once I returned to my true form, I was going to miss having this girl's hair.

"Princess Ana," Jacen said as he opened the door for me. "Thank you for joining me this evening."

"Your Highness." I gave him a small curtsy and entered the room. It was set up the same way as it had been for our first date—with the dining table set up alongside the window. The full moon lit up the sky. Well, it was *nearly* full—there was still a sliver missing.

I returned my focus to Jacen, waiting for a hint that what had transpired between us meant something to him—a kiss, a touch, or *something*. But the prince was as stiff and formal as ever, his silver eyes giving away none of his emotions.

Disappointment catapulted through my veins. Whatever connection that had sparked between us in town seemed to have disappeared completely, and I was at a loss as to what to do to revive it.

"I apologize that I couldn't be more creative with our date this time around," he said, motioning for me to enter. "Due to what happened last time, I thought it best that we remain inside the palace."

I stepped inside, and as I did, he moved back. It was like he wanted to make sure he was far enough away that we didn't accidentally touch.

He was rejecting me.

Instantly, I realized how silly I was being. It had only been yesterday that he'd sent all of the other princesses home but me and Princess Karina. If he'd wanted to reject me, surely he would have sent me home with the lot of them.

I straightened, forcing myself to appear confident, even if I didn't feel it.

"Surely there's more to the palace than just your quarters?" The words slipped out before I realized how snarky they were. "Not that I'm not appreciative of the dinner—I am. I just meant that the palace of the Vale is extremely impressive."

Hopefully, covering my mistake with a compliment would work.

"You're right." He chuckled. "The palace *is* large. But the walls of the palace have eyes and ears, and I wanted to be sure that what we discuss tonight doesn't leave this room."

"Sounds serious," I said.

"It is." He studied me intensely, as if his eyes were x-rays and he was trying to see the secrets in my soul. "And the chefs have prepared an extraordinary meal for us tonight. Let's sit?" He led the way to the table, pulling out my chair. My back brushed against his finger as I sat down, and he yanked it away, as if my skin were diseased or something.

I wasn't imagining it—he *was* rejecting me.

What had happened between when we'd kissed and now to make him pull away?

He waited for me to situate myself, and then took his own seat. The waiters soon emerged to serve us wine, and they placed a fancy looking platter in the center of the table that featured a strange black beady looking food that I'd never seen before.

"I'm sure you have a lot of questions for me." Jacen picked up a cracker from the platter, smeared some white stuff on it, piled on some of the black beads, and then topped it off with some garnishes. At least I recognized the garnishes—chopped egg and onions. "Do you not like caviar?" he asked, motioning to the platter between us.

Caviar—*that* must be what those strange black beads were.

"I've never had it," I admitted. In fact, this was the first time I'd ever seen it. All I knew about caviar was that it was a fancy term for fish eggs. *And* that it was ridiculously expensive.

"Here." Jacen handed me the cracker he'd just made. "Try it."

I popped the cracker in my mouth and chewed. It tasted strange—salty. I tried to keep my expression neutral as I finished chewing and swallowed.

"Well?" he asked.

"It's… interesting," I said.

"You hated it."

"No!" I said, hoping I hadn't offended him. "I didn't *hate* it. It's just different. Perhaps it's more of an acquired taste?"

"Maybe," he said. "But I don't want to force you to acquire it during this meal. So, what's your all time favorite food?"

"Pizza," I answered instantly. I missed pizza like no one could believe. As a human in the Vale, it hadn't been a food we'd been allowed to eat, and they hadn't served it in the palace. Which meant it had been over a *year* since I'd eaten pizza.

I suddenly craved it more than ever.

Jacen tapped something on his phone, and the waiters entered the room immediately.

"Tell the chef that the planned menu for this evening is cancelled," he told them. "In its place, we'll be having pizza."

"That's it, Your Highness?" the waiter closest to him asked. "No more appetizers, either?"

"Do you have a preferred appetizer?" Jacen asked me.

"Umm… cheesy bread?" I suspected I sounded silly— what kind of princess wanted cheesy bread and pizza at a royal dinner? But I loved cheesy bread and pizza. And at this point, what did I have to lose?

"You heard the princess," Jacen told the waiter. "Tonight, we'll be dining on cheesy bread and pizza."

"I'll let the chef know," the waiter replied, and both of them headed out of the room, presumably toward the kitchen.

The prince didn't crack a smile until they were out of the room.

"Don't tell anyone, but I prefer pizza to fancy food, too," he confessed.

"Don't worry." I leaned forward, completely serious. "Your secret is safe with me… as long as you don't judge me when you see how many slices I'm capable of eating."

"I'm afraid I can't promise you that," he said. "Because the more slices you eat, the more impressed I'll be."

"Is that a challenge?" I raised an eyebrow.

"I don't know," he started, and he paused, as if contemplating it. "I can eat quite a bit of pizza myself. And I don't want you to feel *too* bad when you lose."

"Oh, this is *definitely* a challenge," I decided. "May the one who consumes the most slices win."

"You're on." He raised his glass in a toast, and I clinked mine with his. "I already know what I want when I win," he said.

"And what's that?" I took a small sip of my wine—enough to make the toast official—and placed the glass back down.

He looked me straight in the eyes and said, "A trip to the Seventh Kingdom."

ANNIKA

"What?" I sputtered, glad I'd already swallowed my wine. Otherwise, it would have been all over the white tablecloth.

"You heard me," he said. "If I win, I want you to take me to the Seventh Kingdom."

"I'm afraid I can't do that," I told him.

"Why not?" He sat back, looking irritated now. "If the Seventh Kingdom exists, and if they sent you here to compete for my hand in marriage, why shouldn't they expect me to want proof that it's real?"

"The Seventh Kingdom is very secretive," I told him, and my stomach twisted at the lie. Because how much longer could this continue? Eventually, if Prince Jacen chose me to be his bride and we married, he would expect to see the Seventh Kingdom. And then where would I bring him?

I would be exposed as the imposter princess that everyone called me behind my back.

Geneva needed to figure out a way for us to destroy Queen Laila *before* Prince Jacen chose a bride. I knew she didn't want to, but now that Jacen had eliminated so many princesses, we were running out of time.

If Geneva didn't want to do it, I would simply command it.

In the meantime, I needed to say something—anything—to placate Jacen's curiosity. And luckily, Geneva and I had come up with a story for me to go on for now—a story that would be nearly impossible for Queen Laila to disprove.

"It's also very far away," I told him. "It's all the way down south."

"You mean it's in the States?" He leaned forward—my hint at the Seventh Kingdom's location had definitely intrigued him.

"Farther south..." I said.

"South America?" he guessed. "Australia?"

"Neither of those," I told him. "The Seventh Kingdom is hidden in the ice of Antarctica."

"What?" He blinked—he clearly hadn't been expecting that. "How is that possible?"

"Centuries ago, our witches created the kingdom far below the ice," I said. "It's impossible for humans—or supernaturals—to stumble upon. It's a small kingdom, and as you know, we keep to ourselves."

"Why?" he asked.

"I'm afraid I've already told you too much," I said. "I wasn't even supposed to say that… but I thought you deserved to at least know something about where I'm from."

He nodded, clearly thinking through what I'd told him. I hoped he wouldn't push me to tell him more, or worse—bring up visiting the Seventh Kingdom again.

Suddenly, the waiters entered, carrying a steaming hot portion of cheesy bread. It smelled so delicious that my stomach rumbled—audibly. Jacen smirked, and I wrapped my arms around my stomach, wishing for it to quiet itself.

The waiter placed the cheesy bread between us, and we were both quick to dig in.

"There's something else I've been wanting to ask you," Jacen said after polishing up a piece of cheesy bread.

"Okay." I resisted the urge to grab another piece of cheesy bread, since I needed to save room for the pizza eating competition to come.

"Did you not like the cheese bread?" he asked.

"It's delicious," I said. "But we have the pizza eating competition coming up..."

"You're more competitive than I gave you credit for." He placed down the piece of cheese bread he was working on with a smirk. "But if that's the way we're playing this, then it's only fair that we start on equal ground. I also wouldn't want to insult the chef after having already asked him to scrap our original meal. So let's eat one more piece each?"

"Deal." I grabbed for a second piece, since it *was* delicious and I definitely wanted to eat more. "Was that what you wanted to ask me?" I asked in between bites.

"No." He chuckled. "What I wanted to ask is a bit more serious, but it's something I haven't been able to stop thinking about since the attack."

Was he about to bring up the kiss?

My cheeks heated with the thought.

"Go on," I told him, bracing myself for the possibility of him saying that the kiss had been a mistake.

"The wolves were attacking every vampire they came across without a second thought," he started. "But not you. When the wolf got near you, he paused."

"He did?" Panic rushed through my veins—this was worse than I could have imagined. Because I knew why the wolf had paused—he'd no doubt smelled through my disguise and knew I was a human.

"He did." Jacen nodded. "You must have been so caught up in the moment that you didn't realize. But I was behind the wolf, and I saw it. So I have to ask—do you have any idea why he hesitated?"

"No," I stuttered, wracking my mind for any explanation that might make sense. "Perhaps the wolves were only trying to hurt vampires from the Vale, and he stopped when he realized I'm not from the Vale?"

"How would he have known you're not from the Vale?" he asked. "All vampires smell the same to wolves."

"The entire *kingdom* knows the faces of the princesses who have come here for your hand," I reminded him. "Queen Laila made sure of that by hosting the parade."

"And we don't know how long the wolves were hiding within the boundary before they attacked," Jacen realized.

"Exactly," I said. "The wolves' issue is with the Vale —not with any other kingdom. Attacking a princess from another kingdom would surely mean war—not just with the Vale, but with that kingdom as well. It makes sense that they would take precautions not to harm us."

"In that case, perhaps I was too impulsive by sending the other princesses home so quickly," he said with a chuckle.

"You regret your decision?" I froze, my heart dropping.

"I don't," he said, and I felt like I could breathe again. "I meant it when I said I couldn't see myself marrying the princesses I eliminated, and that I had no interest in leading them on. The attacks simply gave me a more concrete reason to send them home."

"So you don't regret kissing me?" The question came out softer than I'd intended. I hated making myself so vulnerable… but I needed to know.

"Never," he said, his silver eyes focused on me with so much intensity that I had no choice but to believe him. "That kiss was the most meaningful moment I've shared with anyone since inviting all of the princesses to the Vale. Why would you think I regretted it?"

"Because you haven't so much as touched me since I arrived here tonight." I lowered my eyes, feeling silly for bringing up such a thing. But it was true, and it was confusing me. I was so wrapped up in my lies that I couldn't be honest about much, but at least I could be honest about this. "You did briefly when I was sitting down, but you pulled away so quickly that I couldn't help but think that you were purposefully avoiding any physical contact with me."

He looked pained as I spoke, and I couldn't help but

feel like there was more going on than he was telling me.

Of course, at that moment, the waiter came in to clear our plates. The second waiter was close behind, holding a steaming hot pizza. Yet a *third* waiter had now joined the group, and he brought with him a pizza stand that was the same height as our table. He placed it next to the table, and the other waiter placed the pizza on top of it.

It was the perfect way to serve the pizza while still giving us room at our table. The chefs of the Vale truly did think of everything.

The waiter refilled Jacen's wine glass, stopping himself before refilling mine. There was nothing to refill, since I hadn't touched my drink other than for the toast. He gave me a strange look before placing the bottle of wine back in its holder and retreating with the other servers.

"There's a reason why I've been keeping my distance tonight, but I promise you that I don't regret what happened between us," he said. "Because the truth is that it's you I want—not Princess Karina."

"Why?" I sat back, stunned. "Out of all the princesses who came here, why me?"

"I knew it the moment you risked your life to save the

humans," he said. "I also care about the rights of the humans in the Vale. Yes, we need their blood to survive, but that's no reason to treat them like slaves. You showed me in that moment that you would stand by my side to fight for their rights. Not only that, but you inspired your guard Tess to do the same. You're *exactly* who I'm looking for."

"Why do you care so much for the humans?" I asked, the slice of pizza in front of me all but forgotten. "You're a vampire prince. Aren't humans beneath you? Aren't they just *things* you can use as you feel like, and dispose of them when you're tired of them?" I couldn't help the venom that came out as I spoke. Because these were all things that Jacen had said about me—the *human* version of me. About Annika. He didn't know that I knew he said them, but Geneva had shown it to me in the Omniscient Crystal.

His face fell. "What have I done that made you believe I think those things?" he asked.

I pressed my lips together, realizing I'd said too much. "Nothing." I shrugged, since attacking him surely wasn't the way to his heart. "It's just the way that most vampires think, that's all."

"Well, I'm not most vampires." He sat forward, his eyes blazing. "What I'm about to tell you is a secret, but I want to be completely honest with you. Do you promise to keep my secret?"

"Yes," I said. "I promise."

"If you want to leave once you hear this and never come back, I'll understand," he said.

"I won't want to leave," I said, since that I was sure of. I was in this deep—I was going to finish what I'd started.

"When I was first turned, my bloodlust was incontrollable." His eyes darkened as he began, and at once I realized that I knew this story—he'd told it to me when he knew me as Annika. "I escaped from the palace and ransacked the village, killing more humans than I can count. If I'd been any other vampire, Queen Laila would have had me killed. But no—I was her chosen prince. The fact that I'd been able to barrel past my guard—a trained fighter—only proved to her that she'd chosen right when she'd turned me. So she kept me alive. She used compulsion to wipe the memory of my face from everyone who had been there, blamed the rampage on someone else—someone innocent—and had him killed in my place. I should be dead. She should have killed me for what I did. I would have welcomed it to escape an eternity as a monster. But she didn't. After all the harm I've done, there's no way I can ever forgive myself. So I want to do what I can to repent. I want to help the humans."

I was speechless, shocked by his confession. It didn't add up. If what he'd said about me to Laila and Camelia had been true—about how he'd been toying with me and would have eventually killed me—then *why* was he saying all this now?

He was either lying to them, or he was lying to me.

From the intensity burning in his eyes as he spoke, every bone in my body told me that right now, he was telling the truth.

27

ANNIKA

"Well?" he said. "I meant it when I told you that if you wanted to leave now, I wouldn't blame you."

"I don't want to leave," I said, this time meaning it for completely different reasons than before. "I want to stay. If you're serious about wanting to help the humans, then I want to help."

Of course, I highly doubted that his idea of helping the humans meant figuring out a way to kill the vampire queen, but I was beginning to get the feeling that Prince Jacen and I might not be on such different sides as I originally thought.

Or was I just falling for him—again—and trying to convince myself that he was the person I originally believed him to be?

"I'm glad to hear it," he said. "And like I said, I *want* you to be my chosen princess. But Queen Laila won't allow that without proof of the Seventh Kingdom's existence."

"This is *your* choice," I pointed out. "Not Queen Laila's."

"You clearly don't know Queen Laila." He chuckled. "She may look innocent, but she has centuries on both of us. If I went against her so blatantly, she would kill me in my sleep and not blink an eye."

"I thought you *wanted* her to kill you?" I asked. "You said earlier that you would have welcomed it if she had."

"That was then," he said. "This is now. Things have changed."

"You're so sure that none of the other princesses would help your cause?" I asked, still confused about why he'd eliminated them so quickly.

"Not entirely," he admitted. "But their main concern would have been fighting off the wolves."

"And that isn't your main concern?" I asked. "It sure seemed like it when you fought them in the square."

"The wolves are certainly a concern," he said. "They murdered innocents—that can't be ignored. But I don't believe that waging war with them is necessarily the best approach."

"What *do* you believe is the best approach?" I asked.

"Talking to them," he said simply.

"I thought that wolves couldn't be reasoned with?" I asked, since that was what everyone said. I'd also seen them firsthand enough times to know that they attacked without hesitation.

The only time they'd hesitated was when that wolf had stopped before attacking me in the square. It had to have been because he'd been caught off-guard by my human scent—it didn't mean that the wolves weren't killers.

"So they say," he said. "But centuries ago, when Laila first came to this land, she reasoned with them enough to sign the treaty that allowed her and her kingdom to live inside the agreed upon boundary in peace. If the wolves could reach an agreement with vampires all those years ago, who's to say they can't do the same now?"

"I don't know," I answered. "Everything I've seen from them has been violence. But if it's possible to reason with them, you should definitely try."

"I knew you would agree with me." He smiled, and my heart leaped at the way he was looking at me—full of respect and admiration. And something else... I almost wanted to call it love, but that was impossible. He didn't know me well enough to love me.

"So that's why you kept me here?" I asked. "To help

give the humans back their rights and to support your quest to reason with the wolves?"

"There's also another reason why I want to choose you." His eyes turned serious, and I braced myself for whatever was coming.

"Why?" I asked, unsure of what it could possibly be.

"Because you remind me of someone I once knew." He glanced out the window that looked out toward town, his eyes distant. "Someone I could have fallen in love with, if she hadn't died so soon."

"Someone from back when you were a human?" I held my breath, since he *had* to be talking about someone he'd known from before.

He couldn't be talking about me—the *human* version of me.

Could he?

"No," he said. "Someone I met fairly recently, actually. A human from the village. She was spunky and fiery, and getting to know her made me realize that brooding around the palace because I'd been turned into a vampire was pointless. She was defiant—she even wore wormwood to protect herself, despite it being illegal for humans to do so. She made me want to create change in the kingdom. When I learned that the guards were coming for her to bring her to the dungeons, I knew I couldn't let that happen. So I helped her escape."

I froze, stunned into silence. He *was* talking about me.

After seeing how unaffected Jacen had been after learning I was dead, I'd thought his caring for me had all been an act.

But from what he was saying now, it hadn't been.

"You seem surprised," he said. "After I saw you helping the humans in the square, I thought you would like that I'd tried to help a human escape the Vale. If I was wrong, I meant you no offense."

"None taken," I somehow managed to say. My voice didn't sound like my own. It felt like I was watching all of this from above—like I wasn't actually here.

Until tonight, I hadn't thought Jacen had truly cared about me when I'd been Annika. Yet here he was, saying the exact opposite.

How could I have been so wrong?

Maybe he wasn't talking about me? After all, I hadn't been wearing wormwood. I never would have done anything so stupid. Yes, I'd stolen forbidden food, but that helped the others in the Tavern. Wearing wormwood would have helped nothing.

It seemed unlikely he was referring to anyone else, but the prince *had* sneaked out the palace and pretended to be human. Who was to say he didn't do it often? Who was to say he hadn't played this trick on others?

There was only one way to find out—I needed to learn more.

"How did you know this girl was wearing wormwood?" I asked.

"I tried to compel her to forget we ever met," he said. "My compulsion had no effect on her. As you know, the only way a human can resist compulsion is by wearing wormwood."

The memory hit me suddenly—of Jacen and I standing together in the attic of the Tavern, and his telling me to forget that we'd ever met. At the time, I'd thought he was a human. His trying to use compulsion on me hadn't seemed like a possibility—after all, only vampire royalty could use compulsion, not humans. Not like I would have known what it looked like when a vampire used compulsion, since I was only a lowly blood slave. I'd never been close enough to vampire royalty for them to notice me, let alone use compulsion on me.

Now it was all adding up.

Jacen had tried to compel me to forget him.

It hadn't worked on me.

I might have thought he simply hadn't mastered his compulsion yet, but he'd compelled those guards in the alley when he told them to let us go. Compelling vampires was harder than compelling humans.

The compulsion *should* have worked on me.

Why hadn't it?

Perhaps I was getting ahead of myself. I might just be seeing what I wanted. This human he was talking about could be someone else.

I needed to find out the truth once and for all.

"Does this human have a name?" I asked.

"Of course," he said. "Her name was Annika."

I shivered as my name—my *true* name—left his lips.

I never thought I would hear him say my name again.

But why hadn't I been able to be compelled? I knew I hadn't been wearing wormwood. Something wasn't adding up.

That was something for me to figure out another day. Perhaps the answer would be in a book. Right now I needed to hear more of our story—from *his* perspective. What had made him say those awful things about me once he thought I was dead?

"Why are you telling me all of this?" I asked him.

"Because I know you also want to help the humans," he said. "I saw it when you saved their lives in the square. I want you to trust me, and telling you this story is the only way I can prove I'm on your side."

"Tell me more," I said, still unable to believe this was happening. "You said you helped her escape. What happened from there?"

"I gave her some of my blood so she could keep up with me and survive the cold, and sneaked her out of the Vale," he continued. "We barely made it beyond the boundary before we were attacked by wolves. We held our own in the fight, but the commotion brought Camelia and the vampire guards straight to us. They'd come armed with wormwood, and despite us fighting them as well, they sedated both of us. By the time I came to, I learned that Annika was dead. She'd been ordered to be drained dry by vampires. Camelia claimed she was killed as an example to the humans—apparently she'd been stealing food from vampires, which was why she'd been wanted in the first place—but I knew better. They'd killed her because they thought she was my weakness. And they were right. At the sight of her corpse, I wanted to take out my anger on everyone in that room. But that would have gotten me nowhere. Instead, I decided I would do everything I could to fight for the rights of the humans in the village. So much needs to be changed in the Vale, and I want to create that change. But if I wanted that sort of power, I also needed freedom. So I pretended I didn't care that Annika had been murdered. I acted nonchalant about it and told Laila that I was ready to meet the princesses from the other kingdoms so we could form an alliance— an alliance meant to help us stand strong against the wolves. At least, that was why *they* wanted the alliance. I wanted to find a princess who would help me further my cause. I've found that in you."

My heart was beating so quickly that I was sure he must hear it. I felt like the wind had been knocked out of me. I was so overwhelmed with emotion that I could barely breathe.

This was what I'd wanted, but at the same time it was devastating. Because all of this lying about who I was… none of it had been necessary. If I'd known Jacen's perspective from the start, I would have gone about this completely differently. We were closer to the same side than I'd ever believed possible. I doubted he wanted to kill Queen Laila and take down the Vale completely—that goal was something I would have had to keep to myself no matter what—but he believed the humans deserved rights, just like I did.

I should have told him I was alive from the start.

Now, I'd been lying to him for so long that there was no way out of this hole I'd dug myself in. I'd lied about who I was, and what I was. I'd lied about the existence of an entire *kingdom*! I was so deep in the web of lies that sometimes I wasn't sure what was true or not anymore.

If I told him the truth now, how would he ever be able to forgive me?

He wouldn't be able to. Even worse, he would probably hate me if he found out how much I'd deceived him. I hated myself for lying so much, and I was the one who had done it.

Yet, he wanted to marry me—as Ana. He wanted to marry an imposter princess from a kingdom that didn't exist.

I was stuck between two impossible decisions.

Tell the truth and lose Jacen forever, or marry Jacen but live a lie.

I didn't want either of those. What I *wanted* was to go back in time and stop myself from getting into this disaster in the first place. But that was impossible—time travel was beyond the limits of Geneva's powers.

I was stuck in this awful mess I'd created. Because even if I continued along as Princess Ana, it was impossible to prove the existence of the Seventh Kingdom. Jacen wouldn't even be *allowed* to marry me.

I would have to figure out a way to kill Laila before being eliminated from Jacen's selection process and asked to leave the kingdom forever.

"You can trust me," Jacen said, clearly unaware of the hurricane of thoughts storming through my mind. "Someone inside the boundary is working with the wolves. If it's you, I won't turn you in. I want to work *with* you and the wolves—or at least speak with their leader so we can try to reach an agreement."

"I'm not working with the wolves," I told him, since at least, amongst all of my lies, *that* was the truth.

"You don't trust me." He sighed. "I suppose I can understand that."

"I *do* trust you," I said. "But I'm truly not working with the wolves."

"How about a blood oath?" he asked. "If you get me in contact with the leader of the wolves, I promise I won't tell anyone about your connection with them."

"I can't do that," I said, desperate for him to believe me. "I would if I could, but the only contact I've ever had with the wolves was when they attacked the square."

And a few other times as Annika—but obviously I couldn't say that.

"I had nothing to do with them getting inside the Vale," I added. "I swear it."

"Okay." He looked at me skeptically. "I know I just threw a lot at you at once. If you have any questions for me, I hope you know you're free to ask. Nothing we discuss will ever leave this room. I promise."

There was so much I wanted to tell him—he had no idea how much.

Maybe I should come clean about everything.

Except he trusted Princess Ana—not Annika the blood slave. Sure, he'd trusted me when he'd known me as a human, but we'd barely known each other. It was far more likely that he'd idealized the person he thought he knew. Once he learned of my deceptions, he would realize I wasn't the person he'd thought I was.

He would never trust me again.

But I wanted to tell him the truth so badly.

If I stayed here any longer, I wouldn't have the willpower to keep up this façade for a second more.

"I have to go." I stood up suddenly, the chair screeching against the floor.

He looked at me in alarm and stood as well. "You're leaving the Vale?" he asked. "Just like that?"

"No." I shook my head—how could I leave when I hadn't finished what I'd come here to do? "I'm going to my room," I said, pressing my fingers to my temples as if I had a headache. "This was all a lot to take in… I have a lot to think about."

"We barely touched the pizza." He motioned to the pie, which must have been cold by now. "What about our contest?"

"Another time," I said quickly.

"Did I do something wrong?" His brow crumpled, as if my words had been daggers in his heart. "You can tell me if I did. I can take it."

I wished more than anything that I could throw myself in his arms and kiss him, and that all the drama between us would vanish and we could be the same people we'd been when we'd first kissed back in that alley.

"You didn't do anything wrong," I said, my voice catching in my throat. He was being so open with me that it killed me to leave him like this. "I'm just not feeling well—I think I need to get some rest. I'll see you tomorrow."

I hurried out of his quarters before he could say any more, not looking back until the doors closed behind me.

28

JACEN

It took everything in me not to chase after Princess Ana.

I'd thrown too much at her too quickly. But I had to believe she would come around eventually. Trying to force her to open up before she was ready would only set back any progress I'd made on gaining her trust.

Meanwhile, I couldn't stay in my quarters for a second longer without thinking of her. I wanted to go on a run through the forest—the outside air might clear my head—but the sun was rising, so that wouldn't be possible.

Instead, I went to the library.

I was determined to learn more about the Seventh Kingdom. I already had a huge hint—it was in Antarctica. There had to be *something* in one of these books that would point me to a more exact location within the giant ice continent.

But I could barely focus on the words as I scanned through the books.

All I could think about was Princess Ana.

Why had she left so suddenly? I'd thought our conversation had been going well. I'd thought she would have been thrilled to learn that I also had the interests of the humans at heart. Of course, I couldn't reveal my true goal of killing Queen Laila—at least not yet. Saying such a thing would be treason. But I'd hoped telling Ana I wanted to work with the wolves and speak with the leader would have made her happy.

Instead, she'd left.

I'd wanted so badly to convince her to stay—to push more to get her to open up to me—but I'd resisted. Because if she wasn't ready, pushing her certainly wouldn't help.

Perhaps I'd been too quick to reveal that I suspected she was working with the wolves. She might have thought I was trying to get her to confess so I could turn her in.

In that case, I understood why my questions had put her on edge. Who wanted to be accused of being a traitor to a kingdom while on a date with its prince?

Then again, I'd offered to make a blood oath that I

wouldn't tell her secret. The blood oath would have held me to the promise—if I'd broken it, my blood would have turned against me and killed me.

Something wasn't adding up. I was just confused, staring blankly at the pages of the book I was reading in the hope that I would find *something* about the mysterious Seventh Kingdom.

Not to my surprise, I found nothing. Eventually, I gave up and headed back to my quarters. Falling asleep would be difficult, but it wasn't something that a nightcap—or three—couldn't fix.

I returned to find a woman standing in the center of my living room, waiting for me.

I stopped in my tracks when I saw her. Her blood had the distinct, flowery smell of witch. She wore all white—a long tunic with baggy pants—and from her tan skin and long, dark hair, I guessed she was of Indian descent. She was beautiful, her skin so smooth that she appeared to be ageless.

"Who are you?" I looked around to see if anyone else was there, relieved she was the only one. "How did you get in here?"

"My name is Shivani." She stood so still as she spoke—like she was some kind of goddess. "I'm a witch envoy from the Haven. All witches of the Haven are permitted to transport inside the boundaries of the kingdoms as we please."

"I thought your kingdom wanted no part in my selection," I said.

"That's true." She nodded. "I'm not here in regards to your search for a bride."

"Then what are you here for?" I crossed my arms, determined to get answers. I didn't like someone magically appearing in my quarters—whether they were technically allowed to do so or not.

"I'm here regarding the feud the vampires of the Vale are having with the wolves."

"You're in the wrong place," I said. "You should go to Queen Laila. She's the one leading our side of the war."

"I'm not in the wrong place." She smiled slightly. "I'm here specifically for you—Prince Jacen of the Vale. I was given an anonymous tip that you're the one I need to speak with. No one else can know I'm here."

Princess Ana. She *must* have been the one to send word to the Haven to speak to me.

It was all making sense now. She'd heard what I'd said during dinner, but didn't feel comfortable telling me she was working with the wolves. Understandable. But she must have believed what I'd told her—about how I was interested in solving this peacefully. So she'd returned to her room to communicate with the Haven and request that they send a witch envoy to speak with me.

The Haven was known for being the "Switzerland" of the supernatural world—they remained neutral on all political matters. If peace were the goal, the Haven was always happy to assist. Anything else, they stayed out of.

"I'm listening," I told her, and I led the way to the sitting room, glad when she followed. "Would you like a drink? I mainly have wine, but I can dig up some beer or liquor if that's your preferred poison."

"No, thank you," she said. "Citizens of the Haven abstain from consuming alcohol. Water will be fine."

"All right." I poured a bottle of water into a glass for her, a Cabernet for myself, and brought them both over.

She waited until I was seated to do the same. I'd never met anyone from the Haven before, but apparently they were aware of the Vale's rule of not sitting first while in the presence of someone who out-ranked you. It made sense for citizens of the Haven to know and follow the rules of each kingdom. Anything else would be far from diplomatic, and the Haven was all about diplomacy.

"Welcome to the Vale." I raised my glass in a toast and took a sip of the wine. "What can I do for you?"

"The Haven has heard about the recent attack the wolves launched upon your kingdom." She lowered her eyes in respect. "Our thoughts are with those who lost their lives that day."

"Thank you." I nodded, waiting for her to continue.

"The wolves didn't believe peace was possible, but your name has been mentioned as someone who would be interested in working out a compromise," she said. "Is this true?"

"It is." I sat up straighter, grateful to Ana for taking action on my behalf so quickly. "I want to stop to all the needless death in the Vale. If that means speaking with the wolves, then that's what I'll do."

I *did* want to stop needless death, but of course, not in the way Shivani most likely thought. I wanted to speak with the wolves so I could arrange a secret alliance with them and end Queen Laila once and for all.

But Shivani didn't need to know that.

"I'm glad to hear it," she said. "The one who calls himself the First Prophet is waiting in the Haven as we speak." She held her hand out across the table. "Come. I'll bring you to him."

"The First Prophet?" I didn't take her hand, unwilling to be transported anywhere until I had more information. I didn't think this was a trap, but it never hurt to be careful. "What does that mean?"

"That's for him to share," she said. "If you're willing to listen to him."

"I'm willing to listen," I said. "But we know a witch is helping the wolves in their rebellion. Who's to say you're not that witch? This could be a trick to lead me into a trap."

She sipped her water, studying me. "I am who I say I am," she said. "However, I cannot fault your doubt, as war disintegrates trust. If it's proof you need, we can make a blood oath. I will swear to you that I am Shivani of the Haven, here to transport you to the Haven so you can discuss peace with the First Prophet of the wolves of the Vale."

"You'll also swear you were sent here on *behalf* of the Haven, that I'll be protected from physical and mental harm while I'm in the Haven, and that I'll be free to leave the Haven and return to the palace of the Vale whenever I please," I added, making sure to be specific in my request. A blood oath bound people to the precise words spoken. It was best not to leave any room for misinterpretation.

She nodded, appearing to be digesting my words. "You'll be protected in the Haven as long as you attack no one—including the First Prophet," she told me. "We don't tolerate violence on our lands."

"And if the First Prophet attacks me?" I asked.

I had no doubt I could beat this "First Prophet" in a fight, but I wanted to hear her response directly.

"If anyone attacks anyone on our land, the tiger shifters will take care of it." She spoke calmly, the threat lingering in the air.

Attacking anyone in the Haven would result in getting pummeled by tigers. Got it.

"Very well," I told her. "Let's make the blood oath, and then I'll go with you to the Haven."

29

JACEN

We arrived in what I could only describe as a traditional Indian tearoom. It was full of bright colors—reds, oranges, and greens—and it had no windows, so I couldn't tell what time it was. But the decor wasn't what stood out to me first.

The first thing I noticed was the distinct, musky scent of *wolf* radiating from the man sitting before me. He stood up the moment we appeared in the room. He was around my height, and he was dressed in the rugged animal hides worn by the wolves of the Vale. His gaze was sharp—strong—although he appeared surprisingly at ease at the same time.

He must be the "First Prophet."

Disgust railed through my veins at the sight and stench of him. I couldn't help but think about the wolves that had tried to kill Annika and me when we'd escaped the boundary, and the wolves that had used their teeth to rip off the heads of all those vampires in town. Vampires might be monsters—I wasn't proud of what I was—but at least we'd once been human.

Wolves had *always* been monsters.

But they'd made that treaty with Queen Laila all of those centuries ago. I had to at least hope there was some humanity in them.

How could I work with them otherwise?

"I have brought you Prince Jacen of the Vale," Shivani told the wolf—the *man*—before me.

If I wanted this to go well, I needed to operate under the assumption that despite what I'd seen so far of the wolves, not all of them were the same. It was hard when every vampire instinct within me screamed *enemy* in his presence—even his mere scent revolted me—but I needed to tolerate it. No, I needed to do more than tolerate it. I needed to *fight* my natural inclination of disgust and treat this man respectfully unless he gave me reason to do otherwise.

Shivani turned back to me, motioning to the man before us. "I present to you Noah, First Prophet of the wolves of the Vale," she told me. "Now that the two of you are introduced, I'll step out of the room to give you your privacy. But just because I'm gone, it doesn't mean the two of you aren't monitored. There's a small boundary around this room, and the tiger shifters are outside of it. If the meeting goes astray, they will take care of it and I will transport you both back to where you came. Understood?"

"Understood," I repeated, at the same time as Noah said, "Yes."

"Very well." She nodded. "I wish you both peace." She gave a small bow and left the room.

I stared at the wolf—Noah—not knowing where to start.

"They gave us food." Noah walked over to the table in the center, where sure enough, two place settings waited for us alongside a covered platter. I had no idea how I hadn't smelled it earlier—it must have been overpowered by the stench of wolf. "Are you hungry?"

"I just ate," I told him, following him to the table. "But by all means, go ahead."

The truth was, I could always eat. But we were here to talk—not to eat. All eating would do was elongate this process. The longer I was here, the more likely it would be that someone would realize I was gone.

Noah removed the cover from the platter and looked skeptically at whatever was inside. "Any idea what this is?" he asked me.

I leaned over and peered in. "It looks like Indian

food," I told him, since Indian food was something the palace chef occasionally cooked. It smelled delicious, and I wanted to dig in, but we had business to attend to. "I would guess a vegetable curry of some sort."

"That explains why it smells like... that." Noah placed the lid back on the platter. "Wolves only eat meat."

I nodded, having expected nothing less.

There were also pitchers and glasses next to the platter. I picked one up and poured it, disappointed at what came out.

"Animal blood." I sighed and looked at the blood in disgust. It smelled bitter and stale—just the thought of drinking it made me want to gag. "I'm not sure how the vampires of the Haven tolerate it."

"I suppose they get used to it," Noah said. "What's in the other pitcher?"

I poured it into another glass. "Water," I said, although that much was clear. "Shivani told me that the citizens of the Haven didn't drink alcohol, but I was hoping they made exceptions for guests."

"You and me both," Noah agreed. "A beer would hit the spot right now." He chuckled, and suddenly, I felt slightly more comfortable around him. From his relaxed posture, I guessed the feeling was mutual.

"Shall we sit?" I asked him.

"Sounds good," he said, and we both sat at the same time, in seats across from each other.

A few seconds passed in silence.

"You call yourself the First Prophet," I started, since it seemed like as good of a place to begin as any. "What exactly does that mean?"

"I was the first of the wolves to receive a dream from our Savior," he told me, all traces of joking erased from his tone. "After me, many followed, but I will always be the first."

I didn't know what I'd expected, but it hadn't been *that*.

"Would you care to explain further?" I asked, having no idea how else to respond.

"That's why we're here," he said, and from there, he told me all about the wolves' dreams and their Savior.

30

JACEN

"So your Savior is ready to rise, but He'll only do so once there are no more vampires in the Vale," I repeated what Noah had told me, wanting to make sure I was getting this right. "And the wolves have a way to infiltrate our boundary, and will be attacking soon."

Noah's story was far beyond what I'd ever thought the wolves' motivation could have been. To be honest, I wasn't sure how much of it I believed. But I was here to listen and learn—not to judge—so that was what I was trying to do.

Listening was the only way I could build trust between us. And trust was the only way we might work together. Especially because there was no way in Hell that Queen Laila would give up her land without a fight.

"Yes," Noah answered.

"And despite the recent attack, you want to eliminate as much bloodshed as possible?"

"Yes," he repeated.

"Why has the Savior chosen *now* to send you this message?" I asked.

"We don't know." Noah's gaze was strong. "However, we trust that the Savior has reasons for everything He does."

"Okay." I knew better than to push his faith, since these dreams weren't something I'd experienced first hand. "You said you sneaked your wolves through the boundary with the help of your witch. But you also needed help from someone inside the boundary to do so. Who are you working with?"

"I'm afraid I can't tell you that," he said. "I hope you understand why."

"I can," I said, since it was true. He had every reason to think I would report back to Queen Laila with information about the mole and have the mole killed. "But what if I told you that I have my own vendetta against Queen Laila and the Vale? That I want to work with you —and *against* her?"

"I would assume you were lying to get me to confess who we're working with," he said. "*If* we're even working with anyone inside the Vale. Have you considered that our witch might be strong enough to break through the boundary on her own?"

"I have," I said. "I've spoken with our witch about it, and know that's extremely unlikely. But I'm not as against you as you might think."

"So you're open to a compromise?" Noah asked. "I assume you wouldn't have come here otherwise."

"What kind of compromise did you have in mind?" I figured it was best to return his question with one of my own. While I wanted to work with him, the less of my hand I gave away, the better.

"Like I said earlier, our goal is not bloodshed," Noah said. "We simply need the vampires off of our land so our Savior is able to rise."

"Your Savior also doesn't want bloodshed?" I asked.

"Our Savior is coming to bring peace to the wolves in the Vale," he said. "It's our decision on how to clear the land of the vampires to allow Him to rise, but I'm sure he'll be pleased if he finds out we did it in a way that resulted in as few deaths as possible."

It wasn't a direct answer—clearly Noah didn't know exactly *what* this Savior wanted. But Noah was the leader of this rebellion. If he wanted to lessen the number of vampires who died because of it, the better. My vendetta was against Laila, and Laila alone. The other vampires of the Vale were innocent.

When I first learned that vampires existed—when I

was turned—I thought they should all be exterminated. I didn't think that such monsters had a right to walk on this Earth. Now I'd been a vampire for over a year, and I knew better. The vampires of the Vale were able to control their bloodlust. Many of them had been turned against their will, just as I had.

They didn't deserve to die simply because they existed.

"What's my part in this plan of yours?" I asked Noah, ready to get down to business.

"I want you to talk to the vampires of the Vale and convince them to move somewhere else."

"That's it?" I asked. "You want me to *talk* to them?"

"Yes," he said. "There's no need for them to remain in a war zone. They can come here, to the Haven. Shivani said that anyone willing to live as they do is allowed to stay."

"Some vampires have already done that," I told him. "But most don't like the idea of living off only animal blood for the rest of their existence."

After smelling the stuff, I couldn't blame them.

"So lead them somewhere else," Noah suggested. "Take them down south, to America. There's plenty of open space there to build a new kingdom. Lead them there, and rule as their king."

"What of Queen Laila?" I raised an eyebrow. "She

won't take too kindly to my leading the vampires to America to start a new kingdom. I could only do that if she were dead."

I didn't outright say it that I wanted her dead, but I hoped he would take the bait.

Instead, he laughed. Full out, head back laughter, as if I'd just said the funniest thing on Earth.

"What's so funny?" I asked, at a loss of what it could be.

He took a few seconds to get ahold of himself. Then he straightened, took a deep breath, and looked directly at me.

"Queen Laila can't be killed," he said. "*None* of the original vampires can be killed."

31

JACEN

"What do you mean?" I asked Noah. "Vampires don't age, but we can be killed."

"*Vampires* can be killed." He leaned forward, resting his knees on his legs. "Originals can't. At least, not anymore."

"A stake through the heart will kill an original, just like it would kill any other vampire." I said it, but now, I wasn't sure if I believed it. It was just what I'd always assumed.

Why would killing an original be any different than killing any other vampire?

"A stake through the heart by a *Nephilim* will kill an original vampire," he said. "But all of the Nephilim are dead. The originals made sure of it."

"Who told you this?" I asked, horror filling my veins at the possibility of it being true.

If it was true, it meant I that even if I escaped the Vale, I would be hunted by Laila forever. As a royal, I wasn't even allowed to come live in the Haven. Royal vampires belonged to their sires, and accepting a royal vampire into the Haven would be a direct opposition to the ruler of the kingdom who had sired them. It would interfere with the peace, and therefore, unacceptable to the Haven.

My lungs tightened, and it hurt to breathe.

"Our Savior," Noah said, bringing my attention back to the conversation at hand.

"Is there any chance that your Savior isn't telling the truth?" I'd wanted to say *lying*, but I didn't want to anger Noah by saying anything too rude about this Savior he loved and worshipped.

"Our Savior is telling the truth." He spoke stronger now, convinced of his words. "The original vampires were smart—they made sure no one knew their weakness. No one but a select few, of course. They wanted to get rid of the Nephilim during the Great War—for obvious reasons. There were surely some lower-level vampires who would have wanted to keep the Nephilim around as a weapon against the originals, so by telling no one, the original vampires were protecting themselves."

"It's not even in any history books," I said, still baffled by this revelation. "At least, not in any I've read so far in the library. And I've read a lot."

"It wouldn't be," Noah said. "Like I said, the originals kept it a secret. Anyone who found out was compelled to forget. We only know because our Savior told us."

I sat back, stunned. This changed *everything*.

"You're sure there are no more Nephilim left?" I asked.

"Positive," he replied. "They were all killed in the Great War."

I sighed in defeat and took a sip of water, needing something to clear my head. For the past few weeks, I'd thought that I could somehow kill Laila and finally get my freedom. It had been the one hope that had kept me going.

Now I realized how ridiculous that had been.

Laila had been alive for *centuries*. Who was I to think I could kill such an ancient, powerful creature?

"You meant what you said earlier," Noah said, looking carefully at me. "You wanted Laila dead."

"It doesn't matter what I wanted," I snapped. "The originals are invincible. So how, exactly, do you plan on getting all of the vampires out of the Vale, since Laila can't be killed?"

"Once her people are gone and her kingdom is ransacked, Laila will have nothing left to rule," he said calmly, as if he wasn't talking about the destruction of an entire people. "And while original vampires can't be killed, they're not immune to wormwood. We'll contain her using wormwood, and our designated contact on the outside will take her away."

"Contact on the outside?" I raised an eyebrow, wanting to know more.

"I can't say any more than that," he said, not to my surprise. "Just that I trust that this contact will keep the vampire queen contained."

If she were contained *and* thought I was dead, I wouldn't have to worry about her anymore.

The situation wouldn't be ideal, but it was one I could work with.

"I'll help you," I decided. "On a few conditions."

"Name them."

"Firstly, I want you to give us one month before attacking, so I have time to convince as many vampires as possible to leave for the Haven," I said.

"Two weeks," he countered. "The wolves of the Vale are geared up and ready to fight. I can't hold them back for much longer."

"Three." I held his gaze, unwilling to back down.

"Two," he repeated. "I inspire my people—I don't control them. I can't hold them back for longer than a fortnight."

"Fine." It was better than nothing—and it was more important he agreed with what I proposed next. "Two weeks."

"What else did you want?" he asked.

"A warning the day before you attack," I said. "And guaranteed safety for myself and Princess Ana of the Seventh Kingdom."

"The Seventh Kingdom?" Noah laughed again—he really was a cocky bastard. "You believe that bullshit?"

"I'm not sure," I admitted. "After everything I've learned in the past year, the idea of a hidden vampire kingdom doesn't seem so far fetched. But no matter if it exists or not, I care about Princess Ana and I don't want her harmed."

"You realize I hold the upper hand here." Noah leaned back and rested the back of his head into his hands. "Most vampires in the Vale are weak from centuries of peace. They don't know how to fight. I'm doing you a favor by allowing you to save your people."

"By encouraging vampires to leave for the Haven —*including* vampire guards who want to keep their families together—I'm making this war easier for you to win," I countered. "There will be fewer casualties on your side as well as on mine. Surely that's something you care about?"

"All right," he agreed. "I'll give you a day's warning, and ensure the wolves know that you and Princess Ana are leaving the Vale and therefore are not to be attacked. But I must ask—where do you both intend on going?"

"That's not for you to worry about," I said. "I'll figure it out."

Truthfully, I hoped Ana would take me to the Seventh Kingdom, but I didn't want to say it and have Noah laugh at me again. Especially because I still believed that Noah was working with Ana.

How else would he have known to send for me when he did?

"Do we have a deal?" I picked up the knife from my place setting. It wasn't sharp, but it would do.

"A blood oath?" Noah asked.

"I'm not thrilled about it either," I said. Noah's blood smelled disgusting enough when it was *inside* his body—I had no desire for that stench to get stronger when it was out in the open. "But it's the best way to hold both of us to our words."

"Fine." Noah grabbed his knife as well, and when he slashed his palm, I did the same. "Let's get this over with."

32

CAMELIA

The night of the full moon was finally here.

Well, it was still daytime in the Canadian Rockies. But the passage to the Otherworld wasn't in Canada—it was in Ireland. And right now, in Ireland, it was eight hours later, which meant the night had begun.

Laila had instructed the other witches at the Vale—all five of them—to uphold the boundary while I was gone. Even combined, they weren't as strong as I was, but they would be able to keep up the barrier until I returned.

I gathered everything I needed and glanced in the mirror one final time. I'd done myself up for the occasion in a black cocktail dress, and had curled my hair and applied a full face of makeup. My wormwood pendant, of course, rested on my chest.

The fae were fanciful creatures. I'd never been to the Otherworld, but rumor had it that it was far more extravagant than anything we had on Earth. I hoped that by dressing up, the fae that met me at the crossroads would take me more seriously.

I toyed with my pendant, nervous. What payment might the fae demand from me?

I shuddered at the thought of sacrificing my memories, like Laila and the other originals had done. I refused to give up everything that I was. If the fae requested my memories, I would bargain with them. There had to be *something* else they would want.

But worrying would get me nowhere. This task was the key to freedom and immortality. The sooner I got it done, the better.

So I held tightly onto my bag—I couldn't lose the items within—closed my eyes, and teleported myself to the crossroads.

Ireland was so stunning that it took my breath away.

The full moon glowed bright and low, illuminating the night. The surrounding mountains were covered in snow—as would be expected for January. But the pond before me, along with the bright fauna surrounding it, bloomed as if it were the height of summer. Bright green lily pads clustered in the shimmering water, and bushes with brightly colored berries surrounded the pond.

Such a contained bubble of life could only be accomplished by magic.

This had to be it. The crossroads.

I removed a bowl from my pack and set to work, kneeling beside the nearest bush and gathering its berries. Once the bowl was full of precisely thirty-three berries, I removed the next item from my pack—freshly bagged blood.

I'd slain the human yesterday in the dungeon. Killing him had been easy—he was old, and near death as it was. He didn't put up a fight when I'd taken out my knife and slashed it across his throat.

He was the first human I'd killed with my own hand, and guilt tugged at my stomach when I looked at his blood. I'd ordered humans to be killed before, but it was different doing the deed myself. It felt dirty—as if I were performing dark magic.

I shrugged off the guilt, since this *wasn't* dark magic. It was simply what was necessary to call upon the fae.

Once the human was dead, I'd instructed a vampire on the staff to bag up the blood and give one to me. The vampire had been confused about why *I'd* slain the human—normally whenever a human was condemned to death, we allowed a royal vampire to enjoy his or her fill of their blood. But once I'd told her that this was an order directly from Queen Laila, she had no choice but to comply.

After all, the fae demanded that the blood used was from a human slain in the recent moon cycle—and the one calling them had to have killed the human his or herself. If I hadn't killed that man, I wouldn't be able to call upon the fae. Then it wouldn't have been long until Laila matched me up with a male witch so I could breed. I would have had to continue using my magic to hold up the boundary, and I would only have about a decade or so more until the constant use of it drained the life out of me.

It had been that human's life or mine. I hadn't enjoyed killing him, but I'd needed to do it to survive. Plus, that human was going to die soon, anyway. By killing him, I'd merely shortened what was remaining of his dreary life in the dungeons.

Looking at it that way, I'd actually done him a favor.

There was no point in thinking about it further—it was already done—so I opened the bag and drizzled its contents onto the berries. Once the berries were soaked in the blood, I used my knife to prick my finger.

"I want to know the location of Geneva's sapphire

ring and how I can acquire it," I said as I added my own blood into the bowl.

I counted thirty-three drops of my blood, stirred the mixture together, and began tossing the berries into the lake. The water shimmered as each one plopped inside. I counted each berry as I threw it in, making sure I'd given the lake precisely thirty-three berries. Once they were all gone, I held my breath, waiting.

I expected a faerie to emerge from the lake, like some sort of mystical mermaid. But nothing happened.

This *had* to be the right spot. Had I done something wrong? Had I miscounted the berries? Should I have gathered them from another bush?

I glanced at the bushes, ready to select another one and start the process again.

"You called?" a melodic voice said from behind me, stopping me before I could choose a different bush.

I turned around, sucking in a deep breath as I met eyes with a man more beautiful than I could have ever dreamed possible.

33

CAMELIA

I STARED AT HIM, stunned into silence.

He was tall, with platinum hair and iridescent green eyes. His icy skin shimmered with the glow of the moon, as if he were shining from within. He wore only trousers, his chest exposed. His chiseled features make him look like a Greek god come to life. He was slim, but fit, each muscle firm and defined. No creature on Earth —not even the supernaturals—had such otherworldly beauty.

I didn't need to ask if he were fae. Besides his stunning appearance, the pointed tips of his ears were proof enough.

"I am Camelia, witch of the Vale and head consult to Queen Laila herself." I held my head high, somehow getting ahold of myself enough to speak. "I have come for an answer to the question that I seek."

"Your question rang through to the Otherworld when you called," he said with an arrogant smirk. "I am Prince Devyn of the Otherworld, and I'm gifted with the rare power of omniscient sight. I can see the past, the present, and the future. Therefore, I know both your question and its answer. But first, I need payment for my journey through the passage between worlds."

"What kind of payment?" I stepped back and swallowed, hesitant. This was the part I'd feared.

"You need not be scared." He was by my side in an instant, and he reached for my hand.

Relaxation filled my body as his fingers entwined with mine.

"What I want from you is simple." His melodic voice was soothing to my ears. "All I request are full rights to your first born child once he or she comes of age."

Relief rushed through me at his request. "Of course," I said with a smile. "That won't be a problem at all."

It wouldn't be a problem because soon I would be turned into a vampire, and vampires weren't able to bear children. But *he* didn't need to know that.

Perhaps his omniscient sight wasn't as strong as he claimed it to be. Because Laila had made me a blood oath—once I gave her the ring, she would turn me into a vampire.

Even Laila wasn't immune to the power of a blood oath.

"I'm glad to hear it." He beamed, and just the thought that I could please him so much filled me with happiness. "Now, although I already know what you want, we must be bureaucratic here. So please, speak your question aloud, so I may verify what you seek."

"I want to know the location of Geneva's sapphire ring and how I can acquire it," I repeated the question I'd asked while preparing the berries.

"I have the information you need," he confirmed. "And I will tell you what you want to know—for a price."

His answer didn't surprise me, since of course, I'd expected as much. "What do you desire?" I asked, ready to give him anything.

As long as my hand remained in his, I feared I *would* give him anything, so I pulled my hand back to my side, needing to think clearly. Once we were no longer touching, the intense warmth and desire to please him dimmed. It was still there, but not as strong as before.

He blinked and glanced at my hand. If my motion surprised him, he only let it show for an instant.

"Your memories," he said, and my stomach sunk at the request. "All of them."

"No." The word escaped my lips in an instant. "There's a lot I'm willing to give, but not that."

"The witches now known as the 'original vampires' gave their memories to one of my kind for what they wanted," he said. "I know you know this—Queen Laila told you herself."

"Of course you know." I huffed. "What kind of omniscient sight would you have otherwise?"

"You're feisty." He smirked. "For that, I *might* be willing to bargain. But I don't know. A lifetime of memories sounds like an appropriate payment for what you seek. Did you know that the fae who provided the original vampires with the immortality spell is a dear friend of mine?"

"I didn't," I replied. Normally I would have left it at that, but since he seemed to like my comebacks enough to consider a bargain, it might be best to throw in another as well. "We can't all be omniscient like you."

"It would hardly be fun if everyone were, now would it?" he asked, although the question was clearly rhetorical. "Well, let me enlighten you about my friend. She has a gift as rare as mine—she's an inventor. She can invent a spell or potion for anything. But her price is steep. She loves memories, and she's been bragging about how she acquired all of those memories at once for centuries. It'll be exciting to tell her that I acquired a lifetime of memories tonight. There's so much value in memories—so many experiences to learn from. People don't cherish their own memories nearly enough." He traced a finger along my jaw, but I backed away, refusing to be coaxed into giving in.

"I cherish mine." I crossed my arms and glared at him. "There has to be *something* else you want."

He tilted his head, as if contemplating it. "Now that you mention it, there is *one* other thing I want," he said.

"What?" I asked.

"Something that belongs to you and you alone, that you've never given to anyone before."

"That's vague." I rolled my eyes. "Care to be more specific?"

"I knew I liked you!" He smirked again and snapped his fingers. "But I'd prefer not to tell you any more until you agree to the deal."

I narrowed my eyes at him, considering his words. Something that belonged to me and me alone could easily *be* my memories. The fae were tricky creatures. They were unable to lie, but they were talented at skirting around the truth. I needed to make sure I wouldn't be giving him the very thing I'd already refused.

"You're not referring to any of my memories?" I asked him. "Or my soul?"

"No." He stepped closer, so he was towering over me. "I promise I'm not asking for your memories *or* your soul."

"Good to know," I said. If he wasn't referring to my memories or soul, he must be referring to an object I owned. Unless...

"Do you promise that what you take from me won't harm me in any way?"

"You will not be harmed," he replied. "I have no desire to harm you."

"Good." I nodded, relieved that if I agreed, he wouldn't be walking away with one of my fingers or eyeballs or something. "Is it an object?"

"Camelia, Camelia," he said my name like a song. "I didn't want to tell you more, and yet I've answered *two* of your questions. You may have enraptured me, but let's not be too greedy now—especially since this is my second and *final* offer. If you want to know about this sapphire ring as badly as you claim, you'll agree to the deal. And if you don't... then I'll get on my way. Although I don't think Queen Laila will be pleased when she breeds you and discovers you've promised your first born child to the fae, now will she?"

I clenched my fists at the word *breeds*, anger rushing through my veins at the reminder of the future Queen Laila intended for me. He'd known while making that first deal with me that it would become leverage for him, and I'd fallen right into his trap.

This deal with Prince Devyn was also my key to freedom. I'd known a deal with the fae wouldn't be easy. But this *had* to be better than giving up my memories... right?

"Fine." I spoke quickly, not wanting to give myself time to talk myself out of this. "I agree to your deal."

"Wonderful." He walked over to a nearby rock, sitting down and patting a nearly identical rock next to him. "I invite you to take a seat to hear the answers to your questions. This story is a long one."

I joined him, and he told me everything.

34

CAMELIA

"I can't believe it," I said, my mind blown with everything he'd told me. "I underestimated that conniving little blood slave."

"You did," he agreed. "But I wouldn't give her too much credit. Geneva did most of the work."

"I suppose she did." I stood up, brushed off my skirt, and picked up my pack. "Now, if you'll excuse me, I have a sapphire ring to retrieve."

I visualized the palace in preparation to teleport there, but when I tried to leave, nothing happened.

"My powers." I stared at my hand and flexed it, then looked at Prince Devyn in horror. "You took my powers."

"Relax." He leaned back and looked at me, seeming mighty comfortable on that rock. "I didn't take your powers."

"Then how come I can't transport myself back to the palace?"

"Because our deal has yet to be fulfilled," he said. "Once it is, you'll be free to leave."

"Great." I rubbed my hands together, eager to get out of here and back home. Laila was going to be *thrilled* when I told her what I knew. "Go get whatever it is of mine you need, and I'll be on my way."

"There's nowhere for me to go." He stood up, gazing down at me so intensely that my breath caught in my chest. "What I'm taking is right here."

"What is it?" I gulped, fear settling over me at how little I knew about my side of our agreement.

He'd known that mentioning Laila's plan to breed me would set me off, and I'd fallen into his game. Of *course* he'd known. He was omniscient.

He'd probably even known that I was going to turn down his first offer and accept his second. Yet, he'd asked for my memories anyway.

Why would he have done that, except for his own entertainment?

"There's no need to be scared." He stepped forward and moved my hair away from my face. For a moment I thought he was going to kiss me, but he brushed his cheek against mine, his lips hovering near my ear. "What

I'll be taking from you is far more precious than your memories, your soul, or even your powers." His voice was low and husky, and he traced his thumb along my arm, causing me to shiver.

I tried to pull away, but his hand found mine, and he held me in place. I realized now, from the hungry way he looked at me, that I'd underestimated him. The fae were beautiful and charming, but they were also dangerous.

I was starting to regret coming here in the first place.

"Tell me." I leaned back to look at him, and it took everything in me to keep my voice from shaking. "What do I owe you?"

"Something you'll find much pleasure in giving me." He entwined his fingers with mine, his eyes dilating as he gazed down at me. "Your virginity."

35

ANNIKA

I WAS GOING to tell Jacen the truth.

I'd been unable to sleep all night, my mind swirling with the possibilities of what might happen. I'd contemplating discussing it with Geneva, but opted against it. This was my decision, and mine alone. She didn't know Jacen like I did. Plus, she had an inherent dislike for vampires. She would try to talk me out of my plan.

But I knew better. If I didn't come clean to Jacen now, I would never forgive myself. I was already regretting not coming clean last night, when the opportunity had presented itself.

After all, he'd told me himself—the two of us were on the same side. He wanted to bring change to the Vale. If I'd come to him to begin with, we could have worked together to make that happen.

This all would have been a lot easier with Jacen by my side.

As for my lying to him... once I told him my side of the story—once I explained what I'd seen in the Omniscient Crystal—he had to understand. Everything I've seen of Jacen has shown me that he's open minded and willing to listen to those around him.

Once I told him the truth and apologized for lying to him, we would figure out how to proceed... together.

I'd downed the morning potion provided by Geneva—the one to give me vampire strength and change my appearance—and had just finished getting ready when there was a knock on the door. Tess. She came to get me every morning to escort me to breakfast. The princesses always ate breakfast with Jacen, although the conversation rarely strayed from chitchat. The deeper stuff had only come out once I was alone with him.

Since Princess Karina would also be at breakfast, I would wait to the end of the meal to request to speak with Jacen alone. I couldn't wait any longer than that.

The less time I waited, the more likely he would be to forgive me.

The knock sounded again, louder this time.

"Coming," I called to Tess, running a brush through my hair one last time.

Geneva was already back in bed as I headed out the

door. The witch sure did love her beauty sleep.

Tess walked me down the hall, barely looking at me. Strange. Normally we at least exchanged pleasantries.

Something must be wrong.

"Is everything okay?" I asked her.

"Yes." She glanced at me, quickly facing forward again. "Why do you ask?"

"You're just quieter than normal, that's all," I said, since if she was going through something in her personal life, I didn't want to pry. "I hope you know that if you ever need to talk with someone about something—about anything—I'm here to listen."

"Thank you." She nodded and picked up her pace. Her focus remained straight ahead, and she only slowed once we reached the breakfast room. "I'm sorry," she said before resting her hand on the doorknob, still looking anywhere but at my face.

"About what?" I'd never seen her act this way, and unease rose in my stomach. What could she possibly have to apologize for?

"Nothing." She shook off whatever she was about to say and met my eyes with a smile. "Enjoy your breakfast."

I entered the breakfast room, and guards immediately surrounded me, grabbing my wrists and cuffing them behind my back.

36

ANNIKA

I SCREAMED and tried to run, but it was no use. There were three guards—*large* guards—and one of me. And with my hands cuffed behind my back, I couldn't reach for Geneva's sapphire ring tucked in the hidden pocket of my underwear.

"What are you doing?" I asked the guard in front of me, still squirming in an attempt to break free. "Where's Jacen?"

"*Prince* Jacen is in the throne room." He snarled, and a guard behind me tightened the cuffs.

I didn't know what these cuffs were made of, but they certainly weren't regular metal. My vampire strength could have broken through that in a second.

These cuffs were designed for supernaturals.

"Does the *prince* know what you're doing to me?" I

straightened and met his gaze, trying to look intimidating despite the fear clawing at my heart. Jacen wouldn't have ordered this. Just last night he'd said he wanted to *marry* me. This must be someone else's doing.

Only one name came to mind—Laila.

Somehow, she must have found her proof that the Seventh Kingdom didn't exist.

"Of course he does," the guard said. "Stop asking questions and come with us."

I tugged at the handcuffs again, so hard that they cut into my skin, but it was no use. Whatever they were made of was too strong for me to break.

"Take me to Jacen," I ordered as the guards tied a rope around me and pulled me into the hall—as if I were cattle. I looked around for Tess, but she was gone.

She must have known this was going to happen to me. *That* was why she'd been acting so strangely.

"I need to see the prince," I repeated. "*Now.*"

"Shut your trap," the main guard said.

His minions pulling the rope gave it a yank, so hard that it knocked the wind out of me. I stumbled to the ground, but they pulled me back up, forcing me to continue forward.

Soon we reached the throne room. The guards pushed the doors open, hauling me inside.

Jacen and Laila were seated on the thrones, and

Karina stood by Jacen's side. She rested her hand on his shoulder—a gigantic diamond ring gleamed on her finger. He refused to meet my eyes.

Camelia stood next to Laila, and she stepped forward when I arrived. "Finally," she said, as if they'd been waiting for me for hours. "The imposter princess has decided to grace us with her presence."

"I'm not an imposter." I held her gaze with mine. "Uncuff me at once."

Once they did, I could reach for Geneva's ring and have her take me far away from here. I just needed them to take off the cuffs.

Otherwise, I was dead meat.

"We checked her when we cuffed her," the main guard said to the queen. "She's not wearing a sapphire ring."

I gaped at his words, and it felt like the ceiling was falling down on me. How did they know about the ring?

This was far worse than I'd thought.

"It must be in her quarters," Laila said. "Send guards to find it. Don't stop until it's been located."

He removed the walkie-talkie from his belt and repeated Laila's orders to whoever was on the other end.

"You won't find anything," I said, since at least that part was true. And even though Geneva was sleeping, she would disappear back into the ring the moment the guards burst inside the room. "Whatever it is you want, I don't have it."

"Liar," Camelia said. She had circles under her eyes—as if she hadn't had enough sleep—but from the way she tilted her head and smiled, I could tell she was enjoying this.

"Jacen," I pleaded, wishing he would look at me. I could barely look at him either—it hurt too much to know that I'd lost him forever—but I had to. "Please let me go. I'll go back to my kingdom. I'll leave you all in peace. I promise."

"Tell us where the ring is." When he finally locked his silver eyes with mine, they flashed with anger. "Once we have the ring, I'll make sure no more harm comes to you. You may have lied to me, but you know me well enough to know I wouldn't lie to you."

My heart dropped at the realization that I couldn't adhere to his request. Because while I believed Jacen didn't want to harm me, there were too many others in this room who did.

Geneva's sapphire ring was too powerful to find its way into any of their hands. If it did, it would be a disaster.

"You might not be so lenient when you find out who Princess Ana truly is." Camelia pulled a syringe out of her pocket—it was full of a cloudy, blue substance—and flicked it a few times with her finger.

"You already told us who she is." Jacen sat straighter on the throne, and Karina let her hand drape further over his shoulder. "An imposter who used Geneva's ring to trick us into letting her into our kingdom."

"That much is true." Camelia uncapped the needle and smiled at the sharp point. "But I saved the best part of the reveal for now."

The guards held me in place as she walked toward me. I tried again to fight them, but it was no use. With three against one, I didn't stand a chance.

The witch paused when she reached me. "I can't *wait* to see their expressions when they see who you truly are," she said.

Then she jammed the syringe into my neck and pushed its contents inside my body.

37

ANNIKA

The cold substance navigated my veins, and out of the corner of my eye, I saw a strand of red hair turn brown. At the same time, my vision blurred, my hearing muffled, and I collapsed to the floor in pain.

The guards pulled me up, forcing me to stand.

Camelia handed the used syringe to one of the guards. "So you see," she said, stepping up in front of me to face Jacen. The prince's face was twisted in horror. "Princess Ana turns out to be merely Annika, a blood slave of the Vale. And not just any blood slave—a well known criminal."

"Annika's dead." Jacen's jaw clenched as he spoke. "You showed me her corpse."

"She tricked us," Camelia said. "She stole Geneva's sapphire ring and has been using the witch to trick us all. She's been masquerading as a vampire princess from a fake kingdom. I don't imagine it would have been too hard for her to have faked her own death too."

"I didn't fake my death." I narrowed my eyes at the witch. "*You* did. You gave Tanya a transformation potion to make her look like me, and then you killed her."

"It's true, then?" Jacen's eyes flashed with pain. "You really are Annika?"

"I am." I bowed my head in shame. "But it's not like you think. Camelia's the one who faked my death—I had nothing to do with that. I thought you were glad I was gone. If I'd known the truth, I wouldn't have come in here and lied to you. After what you told me last night, I was planning on telling you the truth—"

"Shut up." Camelia spun around and slapped my cheek. It stung—by now I had no doubt that whatever she'd injected me with had been an antidote to the vampire blood and transformation potion. I looked like myself again, and I was a human.

I wasn't going to get out of here alive. Even if by some miracle Jacen had a change of heart, I was a weak human and there were too many vampires in here who wanted me dead—Laila included. And what the vampire queen commanded, the guards would obey.

I might as well go out with a bang.

"I came here to kill you," I said, focusing on Laila.

The queen looked remarkably childlike and innocent in her throne, but I knew better. "That was the plan all along. Pretend to be a vampire princess to infiltrate the palace, and find a way to take you down. Geneva's help made it all possible. If Camelia hadn't figured out the truth..." I turned my attention back to Camelia. "How *did* you find out the truth?"

"Let's just say a little faerie told me." She smirked. "Geneva might be powerful, but she's not omniscient. Too bad. If she were, maybe you wouldn't be in this mess to begin with." She turned back to Laila and crossed her arms. "The girl admitted to coming here to kill you. How is she not dead yet?"

"Patience, patience," Laila said. "You're letting your emotions get the best of you, Camelia. You and I both know the girl can't be killed until she's no longer in command of Geneva's sapphire ring. If she dies while in command of the ring—"

"Then Geneva dies too," Camelia finished. "Of course."

"So let's have a little fun while we wait for the ring to be found." Laila stood up and removed a stake from where it had been strapped to her thigh under her skirt, zeroing back in on me. "You said you came here to kill me." She slinked toward me, stopping when she was only an arm's length away, and held the stake out toward me. "It would be a shame if you didn't get a chance to try. So here's your weapon. Let's see what you can do."

She couldn't be serious.

But the intense way she was watching me made me feel like she was.

"That's a bit difficult, seeing as my hands are cuffed behind my back," I said, holding my head high. I wasn't stupid enough to think I could kill the vampire queen in this circumstance. So if this was how I was going to die—with Laila ramming a stake into my heart—then I at least wanted to take it with dignity.

"I suppose that would be difficult—especially for a human." Her eyes gleamed as she twirled the stake around in her hands, like it was a toy and not a weapon.

"You've made your point," Jacen said, his fists clenched atop the armrests. "We're wasting our time here—time that could best be used for other things, like announcing my engagement to Princess Karina." He took a moment to glare at Laila. "Why not keep the girl in the dungeons until you find the ring?"

The girl. His words broke my heart. The way he referred to me was so vague, as if I meant nothing to him.

Which I supposed made sense, given how much I'd lied to him. He had every reason to hate me.

"*I'll* be the one to decide when my point has been

made." Laila's voice was tense, and she didn't look at Jacen as she spoke. "Guards," she said, and they snapped to attention. "Uncuff the human's hands."

They did as she commanded.

My first instinct was to reach for Geneva's ring, but I stopped myself. Because that was probably what Laila expected me to do. If the ring was on me—which it was—she could count on me reaching for it. Then she would swoop in and take it from me before I had a chance to stop her.

Once she had the ring, that stake would be in my heart before I could blink.

I needed to hold her off. The longer I stalled, the more chances I would have to reach for the ring—without a vampire breathing down my throat ready to snatch it from me—and command Geneva to teleport me out of here.

Laila waited for a few seconds, sizing me up before speaking again. "Take the stake," she repeated, holding it out so it was right in front of my chest. "Do your best to kill me. Given that you're at a disadvantage—being human and all—I'll even do you a favor and stand still. I'll be a sitting duck. It can't get much easier than that, can it?"

"You're tricking me," I said, since there was no way she would actually do that.

"Am I?" She raised an eyebrow. "Why not take the stake and find out for yourself?"

She had a point. This had to be a trick, but what else did I have to lose? This was why I'd come here—to kill Laila. I wasn't going to get another chance.

I might as well take the one in front of me.

I took the stake from Laila and held it in my hand. It was heavier than I'd expected—or maybe I just wasn't used to the weakness that came with being back in my human form.

Then, not wanting to allow myself to overthink this for a second longer, I raised the stake and plunged it straight into Laila's heart.

38

ANNIKA

THE VAMPIRE QUEEN'S eyes went wide, and she disintegrated into a pile of ashes.

Warmth rushed through me—starting from my hand holding the stake, and traveling through my entire body. I felt alight with it—alight with *power*. The warmth wasn't just something I felt outside, either. My skin glowed with it, casting its light on everything around me before finally dying down. Then my vision sharpened, easily matching the heightened vision I'd had after drinking vampire blood, and my hearing amplified. Everything was crisper and more intense.

My veins buzzed with a need I'd never felt before. A need to *fight*. Along with a confidence that I had the power to win.

"Nephilim," Camelia whispered, backing away from me in shock.

The vampire guard closest to me moved to me, ready to grab the stake, but I thrust it into his heart at the same time as I kicked the guard behind me in a place I knew it would hurt. The third guard lunged for me, but I jammed the stake in his chest before he had a chance to touch me. Then I turned to the final guard—the one who was still hunched over from my kicking him in the balls—and drove the stake through his back, straight into his heart.

The guards were all dead. But their bodies were still in tact, scattered in a circle around me. The only one who had turned to ash was Laila. I half expected her to rise from the ashes—like a phoenix—but nothing happened.

Her remains were still.

In the time I'd been fighting, Camelia had run up to the thrones where Jacen and Karina were standing. They all stared at me in shock, and Camelia had a phone to her ear. I could just make out the end of the conversation, where she repeated the word "Nephilim" and ordered guards to come to the throne room—now.

I met Jacen's eyes—there was so much I wanted to say to him. I wanted to explain everything from *my* perspective so he could understand everything I'd done.

But if I stayed, I was putting my life at risk. I didn't know how I'd taken down those three guards, but surely Camelia had sent for many more than that.

Whatever had happened to me when I'd staked Laila had somehow made me strong enough to fight vampires, but despite this newfound strength, I doubted I could take down an army of guards. I needed to be smart. I needed to stay *alive.*

Regret filled my chest as I reached into my hidden pocket and pulled out the sapphire ring, still holding the stake with my other hand. This weapon had saved my life. I had no intention of ever letting it go.

I rubbed the sapphire and out came Geneva.

Her eyes widened at the scene surrounding us, horror filling them when she saw the pile of ashes on the floor.

"Take me to the Haven," I commanded her. "*Now.*"

She blinked and we were gone.

39

KARINA

Laila was dead.

The human girl—no, the *Nephilim*—had killed her.

King Nicolae was never going to forgive me.

The king was in love with Laila. No—he was *obsessed* with Laila. He'd sent me here to assist the wolves in bringing down the Vale so that once Laila was weakened, he could swoop in and bring her with him to the Carpathian Kingdom.

Laila's *dying* throughout all of this hadn't been something we'd thought possible. Because the Nephilim were dead. They'd been slaughtered—every last one of them—in the Great War.

The blood oath I'd made with Nicolae said that once the Vale was destroyed and Laila was in the Carpathian Kingdom, Nicolae would allow me a wish on Geneva's sapphire ring. He'd been *so* confident that Laila had the ring.

Not only had he been wrong, but because I was no longer able to complete my part of the promise, the blood oath we'd made was null and void.

If I returned to the Carpathian Kingdom and told Nicolae what had just happened, he would lose his mind. He couldn't think straight when it came to Laila. He might even blame me for her death.

With a sinking feeling, I realized I could never go back to my home. Once Nicolae learned that Laila had died under my watch, I would never be welcomed there again.

When the girl removed the ring and rubbed it, I ran for her. But I wasn't fast enough.

She—and Geneva—blinked out of the room before I could reach them.

The guards burst through the doors seconds later.

"Where is she?" their leader asked, scanning the area. "Where's the Nephilim?"

"She's gone," I said, and then I bolted out of the throne room, not looking back.

40

KARINA

THERE WAS SO much commotion in the palace that it was easy for me to leave. And for those who gave me a hard time—well, that was where compulsion came in handy.

Once out of the palace, I ran through the woods, past the boundary, and straight to the wolves' camp.

A wolf guard stopped me at the perimeter, sniffed me, and then shifted into human form. "Daria," he said the false name I'd given the last time I'd been here. "The vampire who's helping our Savior rise. What do you need?"

"I need to speak with Noah," I said calmly. "The First Prophet."

I didn't think there were any other Noah's in the pack, but one never knew.

The guard led me through camp, where the wolves

were cleaning up from dinner, forging weapons, and practicing fighting. Campfires lit up the night. There were more wolves around than there had been last time—their numbers were growing. A few of them glared at me and growled, but they were quickly hushed by wolves who explained to them who I was.

Noah was sitting on top of a picnic table, surrounded by children who appeared enraptured by whatever he was saying.

He stopped mid-sentence when he saw me.

"What happened?" he asked, his eyes full of concern.

I looked down at my dress, understanding his worry. I was wearing my nicest morning dress, and the hem was dirty and torn from my run through the woods. I'd always changed into appropriate clothing whenever I'd met him at the boundary—the fact that I hadn't changed this time must have made it apparent that I was running from something.

"I need to speak with you." I raised my chin and kept my voice calm, trying to remain as dignified as possible. The last thing I wanted was to bring any more attention to myself than I already had. "Alone."

He led me to a tent near the end of camp and let me in, following and zipping up the flap behind us. The inside of the tent was sparse, with a cloth folding chair, a sleeping bag, and an extra set of clothes.

I shuddered at the realization that this was his *home*.

"Please, sit," he said, motioning to the chair. "And make sure to keep your voice down. Wolves have better hearing than vampires."

I situated myself in the chair, doing my best to make myself comfortable. He sat cross-legged on top of the sleeping bag.

"Laila's dead," I whispered, unable to keep it in any longer.

"What?" His eyes widened. "That's impossible. She's an original vampire. She can't be killed."

"She *can* be killed," I told him. "By the Nephilim."

From there, I told him everything that had happened in the throne room earlier. He took it in stride, letting me talk without interrupting.

"You forgot to explain one thing," he said once I was done.

"What?" I asked.

"That ring on your finger."

I glanced down at my hand, my eyes locking on the gigantic diamond I'd been wearing all morning.

"It's nothing." I ripped the ring from my finger and threw it onto the ground. "With Princess Ana exposed, Laila came to my room at sunset and told me that I was the only princess left in the running. She gave me the ring and instructed me to wear it to the throne room so Jacen knew that he was to marry me."

"The prince never proposed?" Noah asked.

"No," I said. "Although he'd been told of Princess Ana's betrayal hours earlier, so he wasn't too surprised to find me wearing the ring. The biggest surprise he had was when Camelia revealed Ana's true form. He'd been told that Ana was an impostor using a transformation potion—and vampire blood—to pretend to be someone she wasn't, but he didn't know her real identity until Camelia injected her with the counter-potion. Apparently she was someone he knew."

"So you're not going to marry him?" Noah glanced at the discarded ring once more.

"Of course not," I said. "I can't return to the Vale. Once King Nicolae hears of Laila's demise, he'll blame me and come for me. The Vale will be one of the first places he'll look."

"I'll protect you." Noah's eyes flashed with a fierceness stronger than I'd ever seen in him. "I know we just met, and I know that our kind have hated each other for centuries, but I won't let anything happen to you, Karina. You have my word as the First Prophet of the wolves."

"Thank you." Warmth filled my chest at how much I

knew he meant it. "But I need more than protection. I need your help."

"You need only to ask." He moved closer to me, resting his hand on top of mine. "I'll do everything in my power to help you. Just let me know what you need."

"I need to track down the Nephilim girl," I told him, determination racing through me as my eyes met with his. "So I can steal Geneva's sapphire ring."

41

MARIGOLD

I stood on top of the table, surrounded by children gazing up at me adoringly.

"Our Savior sees us, He's watching out for us, and He's ready to rise!" I said, looking at each of them as I spoke. They sat attentively, leaning forward as they clung to my every word. "He's ready to bring peace to the wolves. After centuries of fighting, our time has finally come. With our Savior leading us, we'll find happiness and prosperity. But what needs to happen in order for Him to help us?"

A young girl raised her hand, and I pointed at her to speak.

"The vampires of the Vale need to leave," she said with a smile.

"More than leave," the boy next to her said, his eyes narrowed and angry. "They need to *die*."

"Yes." I smiled at the boy. "They must die. *All* of them must die. We must spill their blood over the land they stole from your ancestors centuries ago. This will show our Savior that we're not just ready for Him—but that we'll *fight* for Him! Once we prove our loyalty, He'll rise and bring us enlightenment that no supernatural race has ever seen before."

My voice spoke the words, but inside I was screaming. I was trapped—an observer inside the shell of my possessed body.

I'd tried to break free. I'd cursed at the demon that possessed me. I'd willed my boyfriend—Cody—to look into my eyes and see that this wasn't really me.

It was hopeless. The demon had access to my body and my mind. He knew so much about me that he'd been able to pretend to *be* me. I hadn't known the wolves for long enough—not even Cody—for any of them to notice how I'd changed.

When Princess Karina had come to the boundary to see Noah, and the demon had spoken to her through my lips, I'd thought she might question how much I'd changed. This person—this *fanatic*—that the demon was making me out to be was nothing like my true self.

All the time that I'd lived at the Carpathian Kingdom, I'd been quiet and even-tempered. I wasn't someone who would call for the extermination of an entire kingdom.

Yet, they'd all fallen for the words of the demon. They'd fallen so *easily.* They were so desperate to believe that a Savior existed who would bring them everything they wanted that they'd clung onto the possibility, not daring to question it.

I continued to speak to the children, brainwashing them. The entire time, I screamed and screamed inside my body. I clawed at my skin from the inside. But of course, it was no use.

I was trapped, unable to reveal the truth.

Because what was coming wasn't their Savior.

What was coming would kill them all.

I hope you enjoyed The Vampire Trick! The adventure continues in the next book in the series, The Vampire Fate, which is out now.

ABOUT THE AUTHOR

Michelle Madow is a USA Today bestselling author of fast paced fantasy novels that will leave you turning the pages wanting more! Click here to view a full list of Michelle's novels.

She grew up in Maryland and now lives in Florida. Some of her favorite things are: reading, traveling, pizza, time travel, Broadway musicals, and spending time with friends and family. Someday, she hopes to travel the world for a year on a cruise ship.

To get free books, exclusive content, and instant updates from Michelle, visit www.michellemadow.com/subscribe and subscribe to her newsletter now!

www.michellemadow.com
michelle@madow.com

THE VAMPIRE TRICK

Published by Dreamscape Publishing

Copyright © 2017 Michelle Madow

ISBN: 1974699250
ISBN-13: 978-1974699254

This book is a work of fiction. Though some actual towns, cities, and locations may be mentioned, they are used in a fictitious manner and the events and occurrences were invented in the mind and imagination of the author. Any similarities of characters or names used within to any person past, present, or future is coincidental.

All rights reserved. No part of this book may be used or reproduced in any manner whatsoever without written permission from the author. Brief quotations may be embodied in critical articles or reviews.

✻ Created with Vellum

Printed in Great Britain
by Amazon